close far away

Pádraig Standún

authorHOUSE®

AuthorHouse™ UK Ltd.
500 Avebury Boulevard
Central Milton Keynes, MK9 2BE
www.authorhouse.co.uk
Phone: 08001974150

Published by AuthorHouse   10/01/2013

ISBN: 978-1-4772-3366-5 (sc)
ISBN: 978-1-4772-3367-2 (hc)
ISBN: 978-1-4772-3368-9 (e)

i

ADRIENNE TOOK A WATER-TAXI FROM the Airport. She was aware from the guidebook she had bought in Dublin that this mode of transport was quick, but expensive. The Sun was already sinking above the buildings in the distance. The Aer Lingus flight was late in arriving in Venice due to inclement weather over the Alps. She did not want to have to search in the dark for the apartment she had booked on the Internet. According to the e-mail from the booking company the taxi would bring her to the steps of the building, where she would be met by a representative who would bring her luggage to the third floor. She did not like the idea of so many stairs, but according to the brochure the view from the top of the building was worth every step.

Somewhat shaken from the turbulence of the flight, Adrienne was glad to have her feet on solid ground. Little did she think that the water-taxi would be as scary as the aeroplane, but that was how things developed as they left the calm waters near the docks and headed into the open sea. A queue of similar taxis came towards them, each of which created a backwash that caused the boat she was travelling in to hit each wave with a fairly loud bang and made it virtually impossible for her to remain on her feet. She was the only passenger and the driver had eyes only for the way ahead. Adrienne stooped unsteadily into the little cabin and sat down on the wooden bench. Just then the taxi hit an even bigger wave and she fell on her back on the bench.

The taxi driver had a smile on his face when he looked around and saw her on her back, her legs in the air, her red miniskirt unsuitable for such a journey. He suddenly became serious when he realised that she was scared. He slowed down the boat and reached a hand into the cabin to help her to her feet. He said something in Italian that she did not understand. Realising his mistake he turned to English: "Catch" as he pointed to the small railing beside him at the wheel. Although he had said just one word of English Adrienne was surprised that it sounded like "Ketch." She asked him was it in Ireland he learned his English,

1

His answer disappeared into the wind as the driver concentrated on what he was doing. The taxi had left the channel marked out by pieces of timber standing in the water, but that pleased Adrienne. The boat was not shaking as badly as they were not now as close to the taxis which headed towards the airport. The tension of fear which had gripped her seemed to drain from her body. The view ahead in the twilight seemed to have something magical about it. The sky was still red from the glow of the sunken Sun while the lights of the buildings were coming clearer into view. At that moment she felt that she had made the right decision in coming here, and thought she couldn't care if she never went home again.

Home was no longer home, of course, but at least she had a place to go back to if she so decided. She had got the house in Wicklow after she and Patrick separated. And why wouldn't she? She had been born and reared in that house so why should he and his fancy-woman have it? He had been quite stubborn about it. He was prepared to let her have much more money, a fortune really, so long as he could have the house. She had refused to yield, although it was in that house, in their bed that himself and his bitch had destroyed their marriage.

There were ghosts in that house Adrienne did not want to leave behind, ghosts of her ancestors. She had never seen them, of course, but she knew that they were part of the house's athmosphere. There were the ghosts too of her own life, of her life with Patrick, the ghost of the love that was once theirs. Right now she felt that she would never want to go back there, but with the passage of time, who knows? Her house would remain an anchor in her life, an anchor she had let go at the moment, but it retained its grip at the sea bottom in the hope that she would return some day. In the meantime she would face her new challenge, in a different city, a different country.

"I have lived too long in the dark shadow," Adrienne told herself. She stood beside the taxi-driver, the sea-breeze in her face, her long blonde hair blowing in the wind as she contemplated the break-up pf her marriage. Patrick had pleaded with her to go back to him, but she couldn't. How could she? Sheila was expecting her husband's child. He could get over that, he said. He could be a good father without marrying the child's mother. It might have been a different story if they had children of their own, but he didn't want that in the earlier days of their marriage. They were too young, he said. They would be soon enough having children when they were in their thirties.

The baby Sheila was carrying was an accident, Patrick said. He had thought that every woman would be like his wife and take care of contraception. The sloppy slut from the office forgot about all that when she was on the broad of her back. Not for the first time Adrienne tried to put the picture of the two of them together out of her mind. The horny little bitch probably didn't forget at all but used the oldest trick in the book to catch a silly old fool.

Adrienne tried to clear her mind of such thoughts. This is why she was seeking a new and different life. She decided to concentrate on the boat, on the water, on the city lights, on the life that lay ahead. The old life slid back in despite all her efforts to forget all about it. "Had she given up too easily?" she asked herself. Had she turned down the chance to raise her husband's child, even if she was not its mother. She might not ever get to be a mother or even a half-mother now. She was already thirty-five years old.

The big question was whether she was still in love with Patrick or not. How could she ever love another man if she was? She needed time to work that out. If she loved Patrick it was love mixed with hate. At the same time if she was to see his blue eyes in the face of his child, her heart would melt on the spot and she would fall in love with that child. Even if another woman had carried that child for nine months and given it birth . . . She realised that she had to let go. The old life was over.

"I'm starting all over again;" Adrienne told herself as the water-taxi moved from open sea into a narrow canal between fairly tall buildings. It was virtually impossible to absorb all that was happening all around her. This was a strange city, a city with streets of water, They passed beneath beautifully shaped bridges over which hundreds of people seemed to be walking. When they entered a much wider canal there were boats of all shapes and sizes travelling in different directions. It looked like a recipe for a serious accident, but as close as the boats passed each other they avoided collisionn. She had never heard of any serious accident there, as it would surely have made world news.

Adrienne recognised the great waterway that snakes through the centre of Venice from the map she studied on the plane. She did not know whether it was a river or a canal, but it was clear to her that this was where the water-taxi had taken her. She realised that they were not far from the apartment she had booked, so she began to gather together her suitcases and bags which had been scattered all over the little cabin by the constant bouncing of the boat on the waves.

The sound of the engine was lower now than the kind of whine it emitted when travelling at what seemed full throttle. The driver asked in English was this her first time in Italy. His fluency surprised her, but she presumed this came from constantly talking to tourists. The taxi docked at a little pier in front of the apartment building, where a teenager waited to carry her bags. Adrienne felt a pang of worry when she heard the youngster talk to the taxi-driver in what sounded like a hundred miles an hour Italian. She did not understand a word that passed between them even though she had been trying to learn the language from a book and CD for months.

She did not feel quite so bad when the young man spoke to her in excellent English, as he refused to allow her carry even one of her cases. Communication would not be too difficult, she felt, if local people had even a little English. The teenager slipped a belt through the handles of the bags and suitcases, and climbed the stairs ahead of her in a way that reminded her of a mule in some old black and white film. She gave him a generous tip. As soon as he was gone Adrienne stood with her back to the apartment door, and kicked off her shoes because her feet were swollen from the plane. She then sat for a moment on the chaise longue, but stood up again in her excitement. She began to slowly walk around her apartment, her new home.

It reminded her of a doll's house. Everything semed to be of minature proportions, the kitchen, the seating and sleeping arrangements, the shower and toilet, the pictures on the walls, the ornaments on the shelves. Everything was small, neat and beautifully crafted. Adrienne clapped her hands in delight as she would have as a little girl when Santa Claus came to her, or when her father brought back little presents from his travels.

He was usually away from home three or four nights a week, travelling from one small town to another, selling men's suits and other garments to the old drapery shops. She had envied him this life at the time, staying in hotels and eating out in restaurants, compared to her mother who seemed to seldom leave the house. She had a much different view years later when she saw some of the second and third rate hotels he had stayed in, places without comfort or character. She thought of the small wall-papered rooms as lonely little cells.

Having neither brother or sister, Adrienne had thought of her mother as more of a friend than a parent. When they went shopping together they seemed to have the same sense of style. As a teenager of course she rejected all of her mother's suggestions, even if particular garments appealed to her. Her attitude at the time was that parents had to be wrong about everything. She wore the most outrageous colours she could find for her clothes and hair. The worst thing was that those choices did not seem to annoy either her father or her mother. "If that's what you like," was their usual comment on teenage fashion. She now felt that her colour sense had to do with her choice to be an artist. Her parents had no problem about that either. If she was happy, so were they.

Adrienne's life had been basically happy until that cruel killer, cancer had insinuated its way into her mother's body at the age of fifty. Perhaps it had been there all the time and had been activated. Those details were of little consequence as her abdomen expanded while the flesh left the bones on the rest of her body. At first it looked as if she was pregnant, but it was death rather than life that she carried. She just accepted it. Too easily, Adrienne thought. What else could she do? Rant and rave? That would have done her as much good as the treatments. She endured some of those at the start, and then put her trust in shrines and miracles. If there was any miracle it was in her mother's stoic acceptance of her fate.

Adrienne used the trick she always used to come between her and the pain of loss. She brought her mother to life in her imagination as if she was there with her in the apartment. In her mind's eye she put her sitting in one of the upright chairs with a glass of wine in her hand. Her mother was shy and would have felt awkward in such a setting for the first time. She knew that she could not push the image too far, and did not want her moment's intimacy to turn into farce. She was not going to start talking to a ghost, even the ghost of someone she had loved so deeply. She just left her mother sitting there sipping her wine as she set about unpacking some of her luggage.

When she had the basics for overnight living prepared, Adrienne opened a bottle of wine she had bought at the airport, poured herself a glass and stepped out onto the balcony. The quietness of the city came as a surprise. She then remembered that she had not seen lorry, bus, truck or motorcar since she arrived. She chuckled quietly at the thought of such vehicles driving on the canals. The same canals were full of traffic, and she could now faintly hear the chug-chug of working boats on the water, big boats, small boats gondolas, speedboats, water-taxis constantly on the move. She thought of the driver whose taxi had brought her to the steps of the apartment block. How many journeys to and from the airport had he completed since? How many foreigners of various nationalities did he meet in a day? She knew she had so much to learn about her new home, this amazing city that was so different from anything she had previously seen.

ii

GIORGIO WAS SITTING ON THE steps in front of his apartment, his feet dangling in the water, his boat tied to the little pier beside him, as he awaited his next taxi-fare. The local hotels were his best customers. They had fixed prices to bring tourists to and from the airport and other destinations such as Saint Mark's Square or the Guggenheim or one of the other major museums in the city. He could lose business if he was not on hand while his boat was free and he was on duty. Thanks to technology his boat was a red light on a screen in the hotel while he was out on the water. The light was green when he was parked and available. He could be contacted at any stage of a journey to pick up a passenger or goods near to a place he would pass. This eliminated much unnecessary too-ing and fro-ing on the water.

The woman Giorgio collected earlier from the airport continued to intrigue him. How had she recognised his accent in English? Could she have some connection with the crowd who would love to find him? No chance, he thought. She seemed naïve and innocent. He thought of her as she fell on her back, her feet in the air when the boat hit a small wave. Not what you would imagine from a spy or a detective, but you would never know. A person had to be always careful. It was a long time since anything from the old life had disturbed him. Things were half settled back home, a tentative peace in spite of the ingrained sectarianism. The likes of himself was still in a kind of limbo. He was one of those taken out of the firing line for his own safety. His death had been faked to avoid his assasination.

He had seen the pictures of his own funeral on the Internet. For some reason it was mainly his coffin emerging from a church door that was shown whenever a news report referred back to the Touubles. Reuters or one of those agencies had it on top of their list, his coffin as well as that of hunger striker Bobby Sands, as if there had not been more than three thousand coffins. There were years between their funerals, of course, because it was Bobby's sacrifice and those of the other hunger strikers that had drawn him into the movement. All he wanted was to strike a

7

blow for Ireland. If anything he was probably too committed, according to some of the leaders. Because he came from south of the Border, they felt that he suffered from the over zealousness of the converted.

His name was never in the front rank of republican heroes, but he was on top of the list of suspects according to the Special Branch North and South. He was not too popular either with drug gangs whose leaders he had taken out, cleanly and efficiently with his rifle. A decision was taken at the highest level in the organisation to fake his death, give him a good funeral and allow the fires he had lit to die down. He had become a liability at a time peace talks were going on behind the scenes. He could always be resurrected if ever his sniper skills were needed. He had vigourously opposed the peace plan because he thought the British Army had run out of ideas, with orderly withdrawal being considered. He had been given a blunt choice, fake death or real death.

He would be an embarrassment to the leadership if it was found out that he was still alive. It would be the last thing they would want the public to know. Most of the guns were now decommissioned, but he knew where his own toy lay in case it was ever needed again. That is why he was always on his guard, from the drug barons and their hit men and women, as well as from his own former associates, now that they had their feet under the table at Stormont Castle in Belfast. They probably regretted not having put him down when they had their chance, but he was too much of a hero among the ordinary volunteers to be taken out in that way. There was no cleaner marksman in the business, with all due respect to the boys from South Armagh. It was a skill he was unlikely to lose, even if he had not taken a rifle in his hands for years.

Venice had not been his first choice of location to escape the old life, but Australia. You couldn't go further from home, and English was spoken there. That is what too many others thought as well. It had become home from home for too many from the movement who had to leave the North for one reason or another. It was too easy to run into someone who recognised you, someone who couldn't keep his mouth shut about the fact that he had met a dead man walking in every sense of those words. Giorgio, as he now called himself had taken the heavy hint, and walked away.

He had chosen Italy because of the Italian he had learned in Rome while studying for the priesthood there. He had come a long way from "Thou shalt not kill" and the other Biblical commandments he had broken since leaving that calling. As he saw it he was fighting for his own people, God's people, the Catholic people of Ireland. Nobody blamed Padraig Pearse or Michael Collins for taking that road, although their hands were far more bloodstained than his ever were.

Nobody ever suffered from any bullet he had fired. Death was instantaneous because of his skill as well as the calibre of his rifle. Their families and friends suffered, of course, from what had become known as collateral damage. They were left to grieve, to bury, to mourn their loved ones, but this was war, every soldier for himself and for his or her cause. He himself had suffered a different kind of death in that he now lived in a limbo from which there seemed to be no escape. He was officially dead, but he was alive and well and working, but oh so lonely.

He would love to be able to go back and take another bite from life, from the old life, the culture, the language, the sea, the life he had lived in his youth. He missed the Gaelic football and hurling games, the people, their wit and old sayings. The Internet kept him in touch to some extent, and it would be a very poor quality of life without it. He had to be careful though, to listen to programmes in Irish only on headphones. He could not afford to attract attention. When matches, currach or sailboat races were broadcast from any of the festivals that took place annually around Galway Bay, it was as if he was back home again. He longed for the day that pardons might be arranged for those volunteers whose situation wwere not covered by the Good Friday Agreement which had paved the way for the present uneasy peace.

Giorgio thought of the old Gaelic saying that sense comes with age. He felt that he now had so much sense that he could not care less about politics, about who was in power and who was not, whether North or South in his own small divided country. The biggest lesson he felt that he had learned was that none of it as worth a drop of blood. Great political leaders like Daniel O'Connell or Michael Davitt had often made that point, but the young blood always boiled beneath the surface and looked for the quick fix of the bomb and the bullet. He thought of the Biblical line that those who live by the sword will die by it also. The same sword of Damocles hung above his own head day after day. Kill or be killed was his motto now if anyone from the past was to discover him, to come after him. It was the last thing he would wish to have to do, but what choice would he have?

Little did that young woman he had brought from the airport earlier think that he had been weighing up how he would kill her if she turned out to be on some kind of spying mission. He studied most of his passengers very carefully. Most tourists took it for granted that he was Italian, but real Italians knew from his speech that he was not. This did not bother them as they were used to fellow countrymen and women who had grown up in fish and chip shops in other countries and learned Italian, badly for the most part, from their parents or grandparents. For all they knew he could have grown up in some Irish or English provincial town, steeped in cooking oil.

Giorgio felt it might be foolish to even mention Ireland in conversation, but most people would recognise that his accent in English was not that of Manchester, Chicago or Sydney. He was pleased that he had come to live in this extraordinary city as he travelled about in a boat that in its handling reminded him of those used by small-time fishermen back home. The big difference was of course the cabin, and the kind of speed it was capable of because of its engine power. Talk of horse-power always reminded him of the notion of a fleet of sea-horses racing ahead of his water-taxi.

He had bought his boat from his redundancy money, his army pension as he liked to think about it. It was the proceeds of a Bank robbery in Kildabhnit on the day of his so called funeral. There was a dark irony in the fact that he had the best possible alibi. He was being buried to all extents and purposes as he held up the Bank staff. He had received enough to buy an apartment if he so wished, but decided to rent instead and keep most of the money for an emergency escape is one was required.

He was ready to leave Venice at a moment's notice, to fake another death by sinking his taxi at sea. Until now it was probably his fluency in the Italian, despite his accent, which had saved him more than anything. Most of those likely to pursue him would expect to find him in an English speaking environment. Either that or he would be in a Spanish resort or a Dutch town keeping an eye on the new Irish wild geese, the drug barons and gang leaders and tax exiles. He was hardly likely however to join those who would most want to take their revenge on him.

He hated drugs and those involved in supplying them. He sometimes thought of seeking an amnesty from the Irish government or security forces. In return he would use his ability as a sniper to take out as many as possible of them as cleanly as possible. He could remain 'dead' as he went about his business. It would give a new meaning to going underground. It would drive the criminal gangs crazy, have them suspecting each other and killing each other. The police would talk of course of the rule of law, and how nobody was supposed to take the law into their own hands, blah, blah blah . . . The streets would soon be free of drugs and the robberies and killings that went with them. It would be one positive way in which his skill as a sniper could be put to use.

Sitting with his feet dangling in the almost tepid water, he realised that this was all a daydream. There would be no amnesty for the likes of him. It was a waste of time to even think of it. He was Giorgio now, no longer Paul. His mother had called him after a Pope, the man in charge in Rome at the time he was born, Paul VI. Needless to say she was proud the day he headed for Rome on the road to priesthood. A typical Irish mother of her time.

Idealism had always been part of his makeup, in both religious and political senses. He was only ten years old when he read a book belonging to his grandfather, Dan Breen's "My Fight For Irish Freedom." It was about the War of Independence in Tipperary in the early part of the twentieth century. He had shocked his father and mother when he returnrd from his grandparent's house and announced: "It's a pity we don't have any Black and Tans to kill anymore."

He had the same intense idealism with regard to religion as to politics as he grew up. He understood well what caused young Muslims of the present day to become involved in suicide bombing. He would probably have done the same at that age. When the day came that he felt his people were being walked on by the traditional enemy he left his priestly vocation behind and became involved in the Republican movement. He already had a good shot, from hunting foxes in the lambing season in his younger days. He had honed his skills in the mountains until the day came that it was acknowledged that he hads no equal as a sniper. If anything his fame among the volunteers had increased since his 'death.' There were a number of entries on Internet sites to suggest that he was the best.

The name and number flashing on his mobile phone told Giorgio that his taxi service was required by local hotel, The Principe. The steward who called told him that a number of American tourists wished to go for a meal in the Academia region of the city. "I'll be there in a minute," he answered, and he was. He was aware that the hotel staff liked this kind of punctuality, and that it tended to mean extra earnings. When he reached the little landing pier in front of the hotel he threw a rope around one of the painted poles which always reminded him of signs for a barber shop at home. Tying a loose knot of a type that was safe and easy to free, Giorgio waited for his customers to arrive through the glass doors of the hotel.

Taking the hand of each tourist, he guided them to a seat in the cabin and made sure they were seated before helping the next person to join them. Most of them were quite elderly but they were in high good humour, and appeared to have quite a lot of alcohol consumed. When all were aboard and the taxi was gliding out into the middle of the canal, Giorgio mused on what a wonderful lifestyle those older people had compared with many of their age who were confined to nursing homes. That was where his own mother was the last time he had contact with his family before his fake death.

iii

When Adrienne awoke after her first night in Venice, she felt she had just had her best night's sleep in years. Glancing at her watch she realised that she had slept for eleven hours, even allowing for the fact that she had not adjusted to local time yet. She did so immeadiately, telling herself: "This is the beginning of my new life." She was just repeating what she had said previously on arriving in Venice and on reaching her new apartment. She stretched herself comfortably on the bed, knowing that she did not need to do anything that day. The bright sunshine through the skylight window told her that this was not a day for staying in bed.

Throwing off the covers, she pulled on a dressing gown and stepped out onto the small balcony to get a view of the city. She realised that she would not even have done that much at home without a cigarette and a cup of coffee. Friends had warned her of the terrible smell from the canal waters in Venice, but she noticed nothing like that. Yes, there was a smell, but it reminded her of the smell from Galway Docks when she was a student in the Institute of Technology there. Family friends had told her parents that she should have attended a better-known Art Academy, but she had enjoyed her time in the City of the Tribes. She was more interested in what she could develop herself in terms of art than coming under the influence of any particular style or period. She had the reputation of being her own woman, and even at a young age she had been strong enough to make that point to her peers.

As a child Adrienne had often said: "I can't wait" for this or that. That was how she felt now. She couldn't wait to visit the galleries, the churches, the backstreet showrooms, anywhere there was art. She was interested in everyone from Tionteretto to Picasso as well as those who came before and after them. She knew that this city contained many original examples of such work, hanging there just as they had painted them, give or take the wear and tear of the years or the centuries. She knew from her glance through her guidebook that there were probably more paintings in churches than in galleries, with free access for anyone who wanted to view them.

The best-known gallery was probably the one named after Peggy Guggenheim, the American collector whose house on the waterfront had one of the most important collections of original paintings from the first half of the twentieth century. That was the first art gallery Adrienne intended to visit on her first full day in Venice. "What is to stop me going for a look every other day as well?" she asked herself excitedly, full of hope and expection with regard to the variety of artworks she was to view.

Whatever about the art on view in the galleries, Adrienne felt that the view from her balcony was as beautiful as anything she had seen in her life. The architecture of the buildings was attractive although there was plaster falling from the walls of many of them, due to the dampness of the city, she thought. Some buildings looked as if they had not had a coat of paint in centuries, the faded pink of their walls giving them a very lived in look. What attracted her most was the fact that they belonged to another time. They had seen kings and emperors as well as millions of ordinary people sail by.

While the buildings belonged to the old days, Adrienne felt that for her it was a good place to start life anew. She was tempted to go back into the apartment for her cigarettes, but it was as her mother was telling her: "Don't. Do you want to get cancer too? Start your new life without cigarettes." She knew that this call came from her imagination, but it was true nonetheless. Wasn't it nice to even imagine her mother's presence and her care.

"As long as I'm in Venice, I won't have a fag," Adrienne promised herself. The next step was to go inside and have a cup of coffee without a cigarette. She found it difficult and awkward, her fingers lost in a sense without their nicotene roll. "Habit," she told herself. "It's only a habit, and a bad one. Do without it." It would probably be just as difficult every time she had a coffee. Maybe she should give that up too, but that would ba a step too far at the moment. "One thing at a time."

Adrienne tried to concentrate on something else, forget about the cigarette. She thought of Patrick. Wouldn't it be nice to give him a call or send him a text to say that she had given up the weeds, that she was happy in Venice so far, and was looking forward to seeing all the famous paintings. That was what she missed most about her marriage, someone to talk to, to tell the little details of daily life, the fully happenings, the silly mistakes, the lttle triumphs.

Why should she tell him anything? Against her will Adrienne felt her anger seep through her bones. He hadn't told her that he was with that one, and she wouldn't know yet except that they had found out that she was carrying hs baby. She had not suspected a thing, thinking they were as solid as any couple of their acquaintance who were still together. How often had they sat side by side on the sofa, his arm across her shoulder as they sipped glasses of wine and watched television? That was exactly how they were sitting when he told her. They had watched a comedy, and after they had laughed together about the screen action and the witty gags, Patrick told her he had something to tell her. Those words gave no warning about what was to follow. She thought he was about to tell her he was planning to go to Paris for the rugby International, as he had hinted a couple of weeks previously.

"We always said that we would be truthful with each other," he began, and even that did not set the alarm bells ringing in Adrienne's brain. She thought he might have overspent in the bookies, as he enjoyed a flutter on the horses from time to time. It never crossed her mind that he was capable of being unfaithful to her. "What kind of a fool am I?" she asked herself, and not for the first time.

"It looks like I am going to be a father," he announced. He waited for her to say something, but it seemed as if every drop of blood had drained from her body. It was if her lungs refused to breathe at the same moment. For the first time in her life Adrienne felt she really understood the meaning of the word speechless.

He squeezed her hand and said quietly: "I'm so sorry. It was never intended to hurt you in any way."

Adrienne reached for a meaning of last resort, anything that would show that what Patrick had just said was not true. He did have a stange sense of humour sometimes: "If this is meant to be some kind of a joke, it is not a bit funny."

"I am not joking, unfortunately. It happened. That is not to say that I do not still love you."

It was on the top of Adrienne's tongue to ask who was carrying his child, but the words seemed to refuse to come to her lips. "I didn't know you were seeing anyone." The words seemed lame, and oh so reasonable, far too reasonable.

"I wasn't serious about her or anything," Patrick said. "It was just one of those things that happen because of drink and carry-on."

"Sure it was only a bit of fun." Patrick did not seem to recognise the sarcasm in her voice, because he agreed with her:

"'That's it. Just a bit of fun. You know yourself. When there is a party."

Adrienne reacted angrily: "You should stop digging when you are up to your ears in shit already."

"It's you that I love. Now and forever."

"Did you tell that to your whore?"

"She is no whore," Patrick said. "It takes two to tango. I am as guilty as she is."

"Is she married too?"

"No," he answered and bowed his head. That conversation had remained in Adrienne's head just as it happened. Each answer Patrick had given was like another knife between her ribs. Her own tongue was sharpening too with every question.

"If she is not married she is not as guilty as you are. You made your vows before God."

"I didn't think you had that much belief in God." Patrick could be sarcastic too. "Maybe you found Jesus when I wasn't looking."

"There are a lot of things about me you didn't know. You didn't know that I would find out about yourself and your whore." Adrienne realised now that she was shouting, that she was getting out of control, but didn't care at this stage.

"You didn't find out," Patrick said, quietly and shamefacedly. "I told you."

Adrienne felt that she had never been as angry in her life: "You told me because you had no other choice, because you found out that she is up the fucking pole. You haven't told me yet who she is. Do I know her?"

"I'll tell you when you calm down." Patrick answered. "I can understand why you are so upset."

"I don't want to know who the bloody bitch is," Adrienne said, even though the opposite was true. She couldn't wait to find out.

"Sheila," Patrick said quietly.

"Sheila from the office, that mousy little rugrat that butter wouldn't melt in her mouth. Sheila who ate at our table, and I went out of my way to make welcome. Did she sleep in our bed?"

"You are all wound up at the moment," was Patrick's reply. "Why don't we talk about it when you cool down."

"I'll take that as a yes." Adrienne fired her wineglass against the fireplace.

Patrick made no comment. He just bowed his head in shame.

Adrienne made every effort to denigrate her rival and enemy as she saw it: "I've heard of men who would be willing to go up on a thorn bush. But Sheila . . . You must have been badly stuck. That little squeaky mouse that hardly opened her mouth the night she was here. She opened more than her mouth when she got the chance." She was silent for a moment, before saying: "You are not serious, Patrick. Tell me that this is just a bad joke."

Her husband had just shaken his head and said nothing.

Adrienne mused aloud: "The mouse that turned into a rat. Have you considered what that child is going to look like? With such an ugly mother. You should ask her to have an abortion. For the child's sake." Her anger drove her to say one thing worse than another.

Patrick sounded worried: "That is exactly what I am afraid that she will do. Have a termination."

"What would the father think of that?"

"I am against abortion in principle."

Adrienne was as sarcastic as she could be: "In principle. Where were your principles when your trousers were down? You are against it in principle, but if she chooses to do it you are off the hook. You will have wrestled with your conscience and won."

"I think that the two of us could rear it," Patrick suggested. "You and I. You have always wanted a baby."

His answer caught Adrienne unawares, but she became even more angry as she thought about it at the time. Looking back at it now from her balcony in Venice, she felt that it made some sense. It was too late now. Sheila had decided to have the baby and rear it herself. It had probably just been a facesaving exercise by Patrick when she was upset and angry. From then on things just fell apart in their marriage.

Adrienne felt she had no real choice but to break up with her husband. His unfaithfullness would always hang between them like treason. Although she missed his company from time to time, she had seen an uglier side of him during the separation. He was greedy with regard to money and property. Strangely enough it was his father that had pointed that out to her the first time thay had met. "You are thinking of marrying a businessman," he had said. "He will always be a businessman, always on the lookout for number one first. You will need to be as cute as he is." At the time she had thought that it was a strange thing for a man to say about his son, but it was true.

Suddenly Adrienne was thinking of her own father, who was not unlike Patrick's in that both told it like it was. They told you directly what they thought. She wondered had this to do with their ages or the backgrounds which produced them. "He will be wondering how I have got on," she thought. Like most parents he worried for his child no matter what age she was. They did not have that much contact, but he was always there when she wanted to run an idea by him, or discuss something important. He had been older than her mother and Adrienne sensed that he continued to feel guilty that she had died before him.

Since he retired from teaching her father gave the impression that all he wanted was to join her mother in whatever kind of heaven they were likely to share. He visited her grave most days, meticiously picking up any stray blades of grass that had found their way up through the pebbles. Although Adrienne felt his loneliness, or maybe because of it, she did not want to burden him too much with her own problems. It was with a sense of joy, however, that she rang him to say how much she had enjoyed Venice since she had arrived there.

"No doubt we will see that in your art," he said.

"You will have to come and visit when I am settled in properly," Adrienne enthused. "The apartment is small but it would do the two of us for a while without killing each other."

"What is to stop me staying in a hotel?" he asked lightly. "That place is full of them. I have seen them on the Internet."

"So you were checking up on me?"

"Checking where you were going," he said, "to make sure that you are safe."

"Well, you can stay here anytime."

"There might be someone with me," her father said.

"One of your old schoolmates?" Adrienne thought he might be travelling with one of his fellow ex-teachers.

"I met someone in the over-sixties."

"Oh . . ." Adrienne realised that he might mean a woman.

"We are good friends, and she keeps me active, but not as active as she is. She has climbed everything from Croagh Patrick to Kilmanjiro in the past few years."

Adrienne did not know what to say: "She must be fit so," were the words that came from her mouth. She had never imagined that her father could be with any woman other than her mother. The world was turning upside down more and more from day to day.

"She has a bit of arthritis in one of her hips," her father explained about his possible travellng companion, "but she is on the waiting list for a replacement It is amazing what they can do with spare parts in this day and age."

"Have you known each other for long?" Adrienne asked, "or are you together for long?"

"What kind of together are you talking about? Don't you worry about your inheritance. We are not talking about getting married or anything like that. We are too old for that craic.

"I'm glad that you have company," Adrienne said, with more conviction in her voice than she actually felt."

Sensing that, her father asked: "But you would prefer if I had male company instead?"

"I didn't say anything of the kind," she answered lightly: "Whatever makes you happy."

Adrienne was worried when their conversation ended. She had heard of older men who did daft things because of their loneliness. They got involved with younger women who were foolish enough or smart enough to marry them and eventually take all they had. On the other hand companionship beat loneliness any day. It was she who had encouraged him to join the retirement club, but she had been thinking of cards and chess rather than women.

She ate a light breakfast, mainly because she had bought nothing, but had a small scone in her handbag which she had purchased at the airport. She was ready then for the Guggenheim Gallery. Apart altogether from the art, this would keep her mind and body cravings away from cigarettes for half the day. It was also something positive to do. She had allowed herself to slip into regrets twice already that day when thinking about Patrick and then about her father's situation.

"This is my time," Adrienne told herself. "They are big enough and bold enough to look after themselves. They can do what they want, and I will do what I want as well." She dressed as well as she could for her day on the town. Wearing a red dress with a small blue hat towards the back of her head, she put on high heeled shoes which she was soon to learn were not suited to the cobbled sidewalks of Venice.

Adrienne stepped on board a vaperetto when she reached the side of the canal. These slow durable working boats ply their trade from one end of the city to the other all day long. They are what a regular bus or tram service would be in most other cities, rugged but reliable and relatively cheap compared with water-taxi or gondola. Aware from her guidebook that it was possible to buy a three day ticket which could be used anywhere in the city, she had chosen that option and decided that she would make as much use of this facility as she could, as long as the ticket, or her sea-legs lasted.

Her first boating mistake was to get on board at the wrong side of the canal, heading away from the direction of the Guggenheim. Deciding to make the best of it and use the opportunity to see more of the city, Adrienne stayed on board, soaking in the views on all sides. "The day is long," she told herself, "and the year is longer again. I have all the time in the world to see all the galleries I want to see." She left that boat after four or five stops and sat at a little waterside café to drink coffee and eat pizza. "What a life," she thought afterwards as she took the next vaperetto back the way she had come earlier.

iv

GIORGIO WAS ON HIS FINAL water-taxi journey of the day, carrying an elderly Japanese couple from the airport to Hotel Principe. It was not that there were not as many flights during the night as the day, but a man had to finish his day's work sometime. He was earning enough to keep himself comfortable, with some put aside for the rainy day or the quick exit. He was tired. The sea had always tired him, even when he was a boy. He had always slept well after a day on the sea. There was a big difference between hauling lobster pots and hauling passengers from the airport, but it was the same merciless, unforgiving sea. It was a wonderful facility, for fishing or tourism, but God help the person who did not respect it. It had its own way of dealing with those who were too greedy.

As far as Giorgio was concerned the Japanese came a close second to the Americans with regard to visiting Venice. They appeared to be quite rich, and it seemed that their colleges and Universities paid great attention to the history, tradition and art of this great city. They were not the best with regard to tips, but they never tried to avoid paying or to start an argument if there was some kind of holdup along the way. He fancied some of their young womwn, because there were so many of them about and they never stayed too long. They didn't expect every man they met to marry them just because they spent a night or two with him. Other women tended to be lke that. Because of the romantic reputation of the city, they fell in love with the first man that paid them attention. How many went home thinking they had been jilted by an Italian, when in fact the man who told them that they had no future together was an Irishman.

Although Giorgio loved the company and closeness of women, he liked variety more than anything' The last thing he wanted was one of them becoming too fond of him. Questions and curiosity were always a turnoff. A bit of fun, sport and passion was enough, each going their own way when that first flame faded. One of the best nights of his life had been with a Japanese girl not five foot tall who didn't have a word of

21

English. He had heard talk of rubber dollies, but it was as if this young woman's body was made of rubber. She wrapped herself around him in every way possible. He muttered to her in Irish while she answered in her own language. It was not that there was much time for talking. He felt that he would not have survived another night with her, but if she had killed him with her athleticism and passion, it would have certainly made for a hapy death.

When Giorgio had finished his final journey of the day, he covered his boat with tarpaulin and tied it up carefully. He went to his apartment to have a shower and a change of clothes. He then headed for the hotel which provided most of his income, the Principe. He liked Jonny, the barman, who doubled as a pianist and singer. He did not look like Elvis Presley in any way, even though he seemed to think that he did, but when you closed your eyes and listened, it could have been the King himself that was singing, alive and well and far from home. It was not unusual to find passengers from the great cruise liners that circled the Mediterranean staying a night in the hotel, anxious to enjoy every moment they spent on land.

At first glance Giorgio thought that such a woman, ripe for the plucking, was sitting at the bar, well heeled, well oiled, loud and brash, in her early to mid forties. She went out on the floor to dance on her own at one stage when Johnny refused to dance with her on the pretext that he was too busy, serving drinks in the restaurant as well as the bar. He was probably afraid that she would be falling all over him. She was pretty enough, and Giorgio felt he could have her for the night if he was so inclined. Stll, with the way she was slurring her words he would only be taking advantage and might be accused of rape in the morning. As it happened her husband arrived to take her to dinner. Another lobster had escaped from the pot.

Giorgio was of the opinion that his conscience had left him at the moment of his first kill. It had gone from him with the bullet that obliterated his target. Until then he had at least known right from wrong, even if he did not choose what was right. He did not know those things any more. Although his rifle had been unused for some years now, his conscience had never returned in the way it used to be. It seemed like an age now since he was the innocent young man who had decided to dedicate his life to God. Was this because of his love for God or fear for his soul? He understood nothing of God any more, and less in many ways of men and women.

He took any chance he got to have a woman with him for the night. It was like a drug, something he needed to have as often as possible. It was not as if he was hurting them in any way. They were mature adults with minds of their own who choose to join him for what was essentially a bit of fun. Was there a rudiment of catholic conscience there still which made him think this was sinful or dirty? The women he slept with seemed to have no problem with that. They wanted what he wanted, pleasure, passion, to close the door on loneliness for a while. What was wrong with that? he asked himself.

Giorgio chatted with Johnny from time to time when he was not under pressure of work, or with Vinny, the resident piano player between musical sets. He sipped grappa because it gave him a quick buzz. He had not liked the taste at first, but like Guinness in his younger days, he soon got to like it. The morning after hangover was seldom as heavy as when he drank red wine. He was aware that alcohol might loosen his tongue, but that mattered little when talking Italian to the locals. If he had spoken of previous exploits they would probably put it down to vain boasting, as with some of Johnny's stories of his closeness to mafia bosses. Speaking English to tourists was the real danger. As for the occasional Irish person he met, he acted as if he only really understood Italian.

Johnny had given Giorgio the impression that there was a chick in the restaurant that was worth waiting for. There were three women at a table without a man between them. Giorgio offered to buy them drinks when they arrived in the bar. He had ferried them earlier in the day to Saint Mark's Square and they had tipped generously. They chatted about the big cathedral there as well as the thousands of doves that mill around the square, squaking and squabbling about the crusts of bread thrown to them by the visiting tourists. Giorgio admitted that he had not yet seen the inside of Saint Mark's church.

"I'm too busy with my boat," was his excuse.

"Too busy for God?" The girl who said it had a twinkle in her eye which suggested that this was not a question from the Bible belt.

"Jesus was a boat man," Giorgio countered, not a church man."

"You should be ashamed of yourself not to have gone to see all those wonderful icons on your doorstep."

"I actually have a book with all the icons," was Giorgio's reply. "I bet I have seen them much more clearly than you did, looking up at that dark roof with thousands of people around you."

The woman shook her head: "A book is not the same as being there yourself."

"I meet a lot of tourists," Giorgio answered. "You would be surprised how many of them there are that see very little as they stand in a queue looking up at a poorly lit roof that is covered in frescoes. I would suggest that a person would see much more detail in a well produced book, or on a television monitor or computer screen than they manage to while being shunted forward by stewards in an art gallery or church."

"You miss out on all the atmosphere," the woman said, "It is not the same at all as looking at little details in a book. They would not have gone to the trouble of painting ceilings without having a purpose."

"Could I stop you there for a moment," Giorgio said. "You have not told me your name yet."

"You do not need to know my name in order to have an interesting conversation."

"I certainly do not want to discuss high art, and I mean high, high up on the roof with a beautiful but nameless woman." Giorgio treated her to his best smile. "We need to know each other's names."

"Do we Giorgio?" she teased.

"How do you know my name?"

"You introduced yourself when we were hiring the boat."

"That is not fair. You know my name but I do not know yours." Giorgio pretended to sulk.

"Kaydance," she said.

"You are making it up."

"What is wrong with Kaydance?" The young woman seemed agrieved.

Giorgio hastened to rescue the situation: "Absolutely nothing. It is a lovely name for a lovely lady."

"You are so full of bullshit."

"You do not know how to take a compliment," was Giorgio's reply.

"I know when a man is ready to do or say anything that will get a woman to go with him."

"Do you think that I am that insincere?"

Kaydance smiled: "I do."

"We should really get to know each other," Giorgio replied. "You may find that there is more to me than meets the eye."

She threw back her head and gave a hearty laugh: "I have no doubt that there is, but I don't want to see it tonight."

"Some other night?"

"I will have sailed. Can we not just talk? There is more to life than a tumble in a bed."

"I gather that it was art rather than pleasure that brought you to Venice," Giorgio said.

Kaydance replied: "Both actually. The pleasure of art." Giorgio began to enjoy the conversation that followed. He learned that Kaydance had a degree in psychology and was taking time out with her friends before starting her professional career.

He could not resist one last effort to attract her to join him for the night: He tried the joking tack: "My degree is in chick-ology, and you are one of the most beautiful chicks I have ever seen, if not the most beautiful. And intelligent as well."

Kaydance's look seemed to convey pity more than anything: "I suppose that is what you tell all of your chicks."

Giorgio suddenly felt tired. He was losing this battle, and truth be told, he didn't care. Even if he managed to lay this babe, she would be gone the next day. Another notch on his bedpost, another distant memory. If she would even be that. The catch did not seem to be worth the chase.

"I have to be off," he said, looking at his watch.

"Out in the boat again?" Kaydance asked.

"Something has come up."

"You are just trying to get away from me," she said. "Just when we were beginning to talk properly."

Although she had no interest in spending the night with him, Kaydance did not seem to want him to leave either. She bought him a double grappa and began to talk about her parents. Giorgio became increasingly desperate.

"You come across like a spoiled brat." The best approach seemed to try and drive her away.

"What makes you say that?" Kaydance asked, surprised.

"There you are, criticising your father and mother, while thay are paying to send you on a round the world trip. Most young people taking a year out would be carrying a rucksack, not travelling first class."

She rounded on him angrily, telling him that she had worked in a restaurant in New Jersey to earn the money for her holiday. Anyway it was none of his business what background she came from, rich or poor.

Giorgio drifted off home to his apartment when he finished his drink. He feld depressed as he readied himself for bed. It was not that Kaydance had turned him down, but that life seemed to hold little satisfaction any more. The thrill of the chase was gone, as was the thrill of sniping, of blowing away real or imaginary enemies. He had fallen between two stools, he was lost between two lives. He could not go back to his own country, his own place, his own people. Perhaps he should move, but did he want to spend the rest of his life running from one hiding place to another, from country to country, town to town, with no place to call his own. Despite his tiredness, such thoughts kept him awake late into the night.

V

ADRIENNE HAD EXPECTED MORE FROM the Guggenheim gallery. It was not that the place was not laid out beautifully, especially on the outside, next to the water. There just seemed to be something lacking, something missing that she could not lay a finger on. Standing in front of a Pablo Picasso original, she felt the colours were weak. Was this heresy of some kind? she asked herself. "Who am I to criticise?"

She knew the picture from reproductions and it had always seemed brighter and more colourful. "Is this one just a faded copy?" she wondered. For safety reasons, perhaps. Most of the Picassos on show there seemed to be from his earlier cubist style. There were some Braques from around the same period, as well as the surrealism of Salvador Dali. Those pictures were smaller than she expected. She wondered was she seeing everything through minimalist glasses. She had felt the same about her apartment. Did a different country give you different perspectives? American artist, Jason Pollock was represented as was Rothko. A note beside a Francis Bacon painting claimed he was British, although Adrienne knew that he was born in Ireland and left some of his works to the Irish State.

She liked the work: *Angel of The Citadel* by Marino Marini that was in front of the building close to the waterside. There was a representation of a man with an erection sitting on a horse. An American woman drew a big laugh from other viewers when she remarked that that guy had taken his viagra. There were a couple of Henry Moore works there which Adrienne liked. She felt a craving for a cigarette as she sat outside taking in the sculptures as well as the view of the canal. She was glad that she had none in her handbag or she would have given in immediately.

By now she was observing the tourists more than the artwork. Well-off, well-dressed, rich or at least comfortable for the most part, with a mixture of students in tops and blue jeans. She admired the way one woman smoked her cigarette with a style that reminded her of a fifties film. Style seemed more important to her than health. Adrienne wondered what the woman's reaction be if she asked: "Will you give me the loan of a fag?" It was hard going trying to do without one, but she had one day done. She had to concentrate on getting through this day smokeless as well.

As she had time on her hands Adrienne decided to visit another gallery nearby, the Academia, but she needed to eat something first. The sensible thing would be to have her main meal of the day at that stage, she thought. It would mean no cooking later. She was not sure would it be safe for a woman to go out for a meal on her own after dark. Anyway she wanted to taste the local food. When she had herself sated with that she had in mind to buy some of the fresh fish and vegatables she had noticed in the local market and cook it herself. It seemed to be both cheap and healthy. Right now what she wanted was pasta in one form or another.

The gnocchi she ordered was tasty, as was the white house wine in the decanter. She was amused to find that she had a certain guilty feeling about drinking alcohol in the middle of the day. "I'm free," she told herself, "free to do what I like. And if I need a siesta afterwards, what is to stop me?" Although she loved the feeling of being free, Adrienne knew that she could not live for very long without company or conversation. She already felt lonely after just one day, despite the beauty of the place and the thousands of tourists milling about. It would be difficult to get to know people, she thought, without a knowledge of Italian. What she had learned before leaving Ireland seemed to be of little use now, as she hardly understood a word that people uttered. The best idea seemed to be to take lessons here. "At least I would be talking to someone," she thought, "rather than talking to myself the whole time."

The little waterside café at which Adrienne ate in the open air gave her an opportunity to watch the passing traffic. The boats were not all for tourists or local people on their way to or from work. There were many work-boats which did not carry passengers, but cargo such as sand, timber and cement. One boat brought the post, another boxes of groceries, barrels and bottles of wine. There were probably others carrying clothes and fashion items, though she had not noticed any of those. It took a while to grasp the fact that the only means of transport was on the water. A jeep or a car or lorry was of no use in such a place. Most of the business seemed to be done, and most people walked on the back streets, on which shops and hotels were also situated. Many of those had an opening on to the water as well.

As Adrienne sat enjoying her meal, the driver of a passing water-taxi waved as he sped past. She glanced around to see who was he waving at, and then realised that it was at herself. She half raised her hand in salute but he was long gone. She realised now that it was the man who had brought her from the airport on her first evening. "He will think I am stuck-up," she thought, before telling herself that she couldn't care less what he thought. There had been something about him that resonated with her, but at that moment she was not sure what it was. It seemed like a complete coincidence that he should pass by and recognise her. The city was so big that their paths might never cross again.

A couple of gondolas came by with all the grace of big black swans. They were beautifully ornate, with a double seat in the centre like a small armchair designed for a couple in love. They were in such contrast to the taxis and other boats speeding by, and it was easy to understand why people thought them to be so romantic. One man rowed each of them with a single long oar, though Adrienne was not sure were they being rowed or pushed along by the oar striking the bottom of the canal. The oarsman seemed to stand in a precarious position near the stern with nothing but his sense of balance and oar to keep him from tumbling overboard. They must have years of practice, she thought.

The gondolas were a beautiful sight. Adrienne felt they represented the style and simplicity of the old world, slow, dignified, quiet because they had no engine. Side by side with them ran the brash commercial, noisy smoky, streesed modern world. The men who steered them were as stylish as the boats themselves. They wore little black hats that seemed as precarious on their heads as were their own feet on deck. Their striped sweaters, mainly in red or blue were part of a centuries old uniform.

There was a young couple, newlyweds probably in one of the gondolas, a couple possibly celebrating fifty years of marriage in the other. "No wonder they call it the city of romance," Adrienne thought, contrasting her own broken marriage with what floated in front of her. She was such a young bride not very long ago, although it was in the Canary Islands that she and Patrick had honeymooned. They had chosen Lanzerote because she had heard that the light was so good for painting. It all seemed like a different life now, another world.

Did anybody know what life held for this young couple either? Had the old couple's hearts been broken a few times along the way? "Maybe she is not his wife at all," she thought, as the boat floated closer. The woman certainly looked much younger than her companion now.

Adrienne raised her hand in a greeting, or a blessing maybe as the gondolas came close. "They are happy today," she mused. "Isn't that enough for now." Maybe the day would come when I well be happy with someone too."

There were so many pictures in the Gailearaí dell Academia that Adrienne walked around the whole place three times to get a flavour of them all. After all that she knew that she only had glanced at most of them. She knew that she would be returning here again and again, because it appealed to her in a way that the Guggenheim had not. She intended to go back there too, of course, to see if it appealed to her more when she was well rested.

As she looked around now, she thought that there must be a condition known as blinded by art. It reminded her in a way of being in a beautiful place in the West of Ireland, hills, mountains, lakes and sea in whatever direction you looked, so much beauty before you that you would be afraid that you were missing something. She reminded herself that: "this place will still be here tomorrow and the next day and the day after. I will have plenty of time to savour all its beauty."

Adrienne had intended to start painting again in a month or two, hoping to be inspired by the art she would have viewed in all the various galleries and churches in the meantime. For the beginning at least she intended not to spend full days painting as she had in the past, something which eventually wore her out and led her to feel that she was losing her way as an artist. "A couple of hours in the morning," she told herself, "and the rest of the day for myself."

She had once heard the late great Irish writer John McGahern being interviewed on radio. He had explained that was how he worked: a couple of hours writing in the morning and the rest of the day on his farm dealing with whatever the day brought. Having read many of his books, Adrienne thought this was certainly an effective way to work, in his case anyway. She wondered would she have enough self-discipline to stick to that kind of schedeule. A person would need to be flexible. You could not just down your brush while full of inspiration. The other side of the story was that work done while over-tired was often a waste of time.

There were obviously days in everyone's life when nothing got done without effort, pain and sweat. Work would begin in the knowledge that a person was quite likely to make a mess of it. But the effort was put in to it, and somewhere when you least expected a new idea or inspiration would spring from it. It would be followed by a day on which you would think that an angel sat on your shoulder, that every stroke came easier than the previous one, and you had a picture to prove it. She thought of the many artists represented in that gallery which contained centuries of paintings. How many were artisans carrying out the wishes of a major artist, or the commission of some merchant or Pope. More perspiration than inspiration in many cases probably.

Adrienne felt that much depended on an artist's humour on any particular day. On the amount of sleep a person had, on their period, their hormones, on difficulties in life. Strangely enough it it was when life was dark and seemingly hopeless at the time of her break-up with Patrick that she had done some of her best work. It was as if all the anger and hate and disillusion and loneliness inside her was being translated on to the canvas. She herself felt that the paintings were dark and brooding. Despite that many critics had remarked on the boldness of her colours and the freedom of her brush strokes.

Adrienne smiled to herself on viewing some paintings with religious themes in one of the side galleries. It was not that they were not well painted, but they reflected more the vanity of their sponsors than the themes they represented. There was one crucifixion scene poignantly painted in so far as the Christ figure, Mary and John were concerned, but who was the other figure? Some Cardinal from the sixteenth century who had obviously paid for the painting and had himself included at the coalface of life and death. A bigwig celebrity of the time had seen to it that he would be at the Lord's right hand in this life at least. It was a shame that this took away from what was a genuinely good crucifixion scene, full of life and feeling. There were so many paintings with similar themes that Adrienne had a reel in her head looking at them all. She was pleased when she reached the area which contained the icons from Byzanthium.

These had a great room all to themselves, and Adrienne felt that she had never been surrounded with so much gold paint. The lighting suited the pictures in that there was not any glow or reflection from the rich paint. Adrienne thought that the shape and look on many of the faces were not unlike modern art. They could have been drawn by Picasso on a slow day, she reflected with some amusement. She had heard somewhere that most icons were painted, not so much to look at, but to think that Jesus, Mary, Joseph and other saints were looking at you. She was not sure what was meant by that, but it seemed like a nice idea.

Reading the brochures about the gallery, Adrienne learned that it was in the time of Napoleon that many of the religious pictures had been gathered under one roof to prevent their destruction in churches he had ordered to be closed down. "It's an ill wind," she thought. Much of the work might have been lost or damaged by neglect, dampness or being motheaten only for the orders of the Emperor, even if those were for the wrong reasons. It was hard to believe now that Venice once had its own empire which lasted for centuries, and that the entity called Italy was relatively new, something like a hundred and fifty years old.

There were pictures and statues of lions all over the place, the lion being the traditional symbol of Saint Mark who was long associated with Venice. The evangelist was mentioned in the title of the picture: *The Translation of the Body of Saint Mark* by Tiontoretto. Adrienne had heard of painters such as Bellini who were represented in the Academia, but never of Carpachio or Martegna, although they were obviously held in high regard in that part of the world. Generally speaking the day had such an effect on her that she thought as she sailed home in the vaperetto that it would not be long before she had a paintbrush in her hand again.

vi

THE THING GIORGIO LIKED BEST about his work was that it was never boring. He was on his way to the airport in the morning, to the Lido in the afternoon, to Saint Mark's Square or to one of the cruiseliners in the evening. He met different people all the time and seldom met the same person twice. An exception was the woman he has spotted in the waterside café as he sped past. It was the same woman who had landed on her backside in the cabin of his taxi with her legs in the air. It was an image that stayed in his mind even though he was trying to blot all the women of the world from his consciousness. "A waste of time," he told himself. "She would have no interest in me." She had pretended not to notice as he drove past the café and had not even lifted a hand when he waved. It was as if he was not there at all. "Her loss . . ." He was fed up with all women.

As Giorgio manouvered his taxi through the waters of the canal he was thinking seriously about his life. Maybe he was long enough in this place, but where was he to find work that appealed to him so much? It was good cover too, given his background. Who would expect to find a republican former sniper speaking Italian and driving a Venetian water-taxi? He admitted to himself that he was satisfied in his work but not with his life. It was ok to have a good time with different women for a while. It was probably every man's secret dream—have your pleasure with no complications. The operative words though were 'for a while.' There was no lasting satifaction.

For a while was alright for a teenager or a young man in his twenties, but there was a desire for something more permanent as you got older. It was said that women had biological clocks that told them when they needed to have children before it was too late. Giorgio felt that such a clock ticked inside himself, not unlike the clocks that ticked in the oldfashioned bombs that older comrades manufactured before the newer technoligies made them redundant. The words: "My old alarm clock" went through his mind as he remembered a dramatic version of

Brendan Behan's "Borstal Boy" he had seen on stage in Dublin's Abbey Theatre many years earlier.

Giorgio was aware however that getting into a longterm relationship with a woman could be a sentence of death for both of them. She would want to know everything about him, and rightly so. Would she be able to keep her mouth shut when she was with her friends, when all of them had more than enough to drink? What woman would want to be with him when she found out about his background? The knowledge that he had killed people in cold blood would chill most prospective girlfriends. Who would want to live with such a man?

There was an old saying he remembered from his youth when dogs were worrying sheep that the dog that killed once would kill again. It had to be put down even if was a favourite pet. The same was probably true with regard to himself. He would kill again if he had to. It was not as if he ever wanted to do so, but he might need to if any of them came after him. It was a kill or be killed situation, and self preservation and self defence were among the most natural human instincts.

Giorgio remembered the satisfaction that came with a clean kill. It was not that he enjoyed the taking of a life, but he revelled in the skill involved. At that moment the feeling was as good or better than sex. The problem was that you could not hang around to enjoy it. Police and soldiers would be on your case in a matter of minutes. The image of police plodders sometimes portrayed in television dramas was the opposite to the truth. They were professional to their fingertips. After a hit you needed to be out of there in a matter of seconds or they would be on to you.

He prided himself in the fact that he was a professional too. He would have his plans meticiously made, his escape route mapped out, his rifle smuggled away by a diligint comrade. In a city situation he would walk down the street in a suit, collar and tie, looking like a banker or a civil servant. He would feign surprise at what had happened, as if he was as shocked as the next person. Being in the open, near the scene was usually the safest place to be in the immediate aftermath of such a shooting. The big danger was that you would be caught on CCTV too often in such circumstances, but a subtle change of appearance, the wearing of a hat, spectacles or a beard was usually enough to throw people off the scent.

He missed the adrenalin rush that came with the kill. He didn't like to think of himself actually enjoying killing another human being, but this was war. He told himself that the part he really enjoyed was using his skill when this led to a successful outcome. Those times could not be brought back, those thrills, the mixture of anticipation, excitement and fear. The only place he could get that now was by joining some mercenery group in Africa. Did he want to fight for some cause that was not dear to his own heart? Would he get the opportunity to work as a sniper, or would he end up trudging from village to village terrifying the residents?

Even when he was in the movement, Giorgio felt that he was more a gun for hire than one of the lads, one of the club. That may have been because he was not from the North, and there was always a fear of infilttration by spies or agents working for the British or Irish governments. Some of the leaders felt that he did not really understand things that were part of their culture, that he had not experienced the indignity of internment without trial, of body searches, of house searches, of being an alien in your own country. He was given specific jobs and hurried back over the border again. When he was funeraled, as some of them put it, the door was left open in case his skills were needed again. That was why he was not just blown away. They would not be sending for him now that they were cosying up to the old enemy in Stormont Castle.

Giorgio had an extremely busy but productive day as a great liner with thousands of passengers had dropped anchor at the mouth of the bay. She was too big to dock, so boats of all kinds gathered around like bees to a honeypot to take passengers ashore. He had little time now to think about past or present problems as he ferried rich tourists to their overnight destinations. By the time he finished he had a pocketfull of tips apart from normal charges, so he decided to go to the Principe for dinner.

His mates there, Johnny and Vinny teased him because he did not seem interested in any woman at the bar. They suggested that he must have a 'little bird' hidden somewhere. They continued to banter, even though Giorgio always found it difficult to joke properly in a learned language. He sat on one of the ornate chairs sipping a beer and listening to the music and songs until nearly mdnight. As he made his way home he felt fairly contented after a satisfactory day's work.

As he lay in bed and waited for sleep to creep up on him Giorgio reflected on whether too much alcohol contributed to the dark moods he had experienced recently. Perhaps the grappa was too strong, that he would be better off sticking to beer or wine. The couple of beers earlier had been light and pleasant, and compared with earlier in the day he thought he might spend the rest of his life in Venice. The work was satisfying, the money good, as was the bit of fun with friends in the bar. He smiled to himself as he thought that he had not really given up on all women.

He decided that he would make an effort to meet that woman who had fallen in his boat, and whose face continued to haunt him in a good kind of way. There was something extremely attractive about her that he could not quite put a finger on. Who was she? What had brought her to Venice? Why had she so much luggage? What about that big square box of a type he had seen painters carry? He knew where she was staying. He had brought her to the steps of the building. What had he to lose by trying to meet her? He knew that his taxi would happen to be passing that doorway the following day, and that thought led to pleasant sleep.

vii

ADRIENNE SET OUT FOR PADOVA the following morning. She had seen the placename on the map a couple of times without taking much notice of it. The thought struck then that this was what was called Padua in Englsh, a place long associated with the saint, Anthony of Padua. She decided to visit the shrine as a mark of respect to her mother who had a great devotion to: "Saint Anthony." Anytime there was something lost or missing, he was the saint who was given the task of retrieving it. As a child she had imagined that Anthony was involved in some sort of game of hide and seek. He was constantly hiding things, which made it all the easier for him to find them again.

She now looked at turning to a saint for help was more of a superstition than anything else, but she still called on Anthony when her keys were missing or she could not find the size of brush she needed for her painting. The curses of frustration came first, of course, to be followed by reluctant prayer. Whether it was an accident or in some way psychological, Adrienne felt that in practice she had never been let down by Saint Anthony. It would bring her closer to her mother in some way, she felt, to visit the shrine of the saint and pass on both of their thanks.

It came as a surprise to find how cheap a return train ticket from Venice to Padua cost, slightly less than five euro. Adrienne sat on a high modern seat with an excellent view of the surrounding scenery. They crossed an expanse of sea at first on a kind of bridge-road which seemed to be just a couple of metres above the water. This gave her a much better view of the receding city than she had on her first evening there, as the boat had bounced continuously on the small waves. The part of the city outskirts the train entered then was far less magical than the picture postcard bridges, buildings and canals she had become used to.

The train passed through great industrial wastelands that reminded her of a trip she had taken from Frankfurt to Baden-Baden when she had a small exhibition there as part of a German-Irish festival. Both areas looked as if they had been bombed and just left there, but it was far more likely to be unemployment and neglect that had led to their sorry state. They were suddenly passing through what seemed like market gardening country, full of neat, well-tilled fields with vegetables of every kind. It surprised Adrienne that she did not notice any vines, but perhaps this was not a wine-growing area. They were in Padua railway station before she had settled properly in her seat.

The taxi from the station to to the shrine of the saint was more expensive than the train-fare, but it was worth it in that she had no idea of how to get there by bus. The big Mercedes seemed to float along the streets until they reached the Basilica which contains the body and other relics of the saint. "San Antoin," the taxi-man called it which reminded Adrienne of a Johnny Cash song much loved by her father. As soon as she saw the great church and the many pilgrims that surrounded it, she realised that far more than her late mother loved this saint. There seemed to be people there of every age, shape and size and nation, rich and poor, fit, lame, handicapped, black, white and yellow.

"If this is superstition," Adrienne thought, "there is an awful lot of it around." Inside the great Basilica a long queue of people walked past the tomb of the saint. Each person paused or a moment to place a hand on the black marble, before moving on. Adrienne took her place in the line and waited patiently for her turn. The phrase: "The poor and the sick and the blind and the lame" ran through her mind. It was not that everyone was poor, but it was a place that made room for the poor. She held her hand against the cold stone, in her mother's memory and for herself as well, and whatever life had in store for her. Then she thought of her father and had an almost uncontrollable urge to laugh which she stifled with her hand. "Maybe he will bring his pensioner bimbo here," she smiled. Her mother might not approve of what Saint Anthony had found for him.

"What would Patrick say if he saw her in such a place?" Adrienne could imagine him saying: "Desperate" again and again. As far as she knew he had not darkened the door of a church since the day they married. This, however was not the place for complaints or regrets. What had happened, happened. She did not like it but would have to put it behind her. Almost in spite of herself she asked the saint to look after the man who had been her husband, who still was, officially.

The idea of praying for his child and the woman who carried it stuck in her throat, but she forced herself to do it in this place. Adrienne knew in her heart that it was a good thing to let go of the pain and the heartbreak, and the life that was past. If she did not do so here in a place she felt herself to be in the presence of holiness, she would probably never do so. It was not that the pain and loss and anger would not be there again the next day, but right now it was: "one day at a time."

As she wandered from one great porch to another, Adrienne felt light-headed. It was as if a weight had been lifted from her shoulders. It was probably just psychological, she told herself, but that did not matter. It was real for now at least. She looked at the many pictures and paintings in the buildings, few enough of which seemed to be of good quality, but they reflected centuries of faith, the faith mainly of the poor, even if the pictures had been painted for the rich.

There were samples too of clothes and vestments worn by Anthony himself seven hundred years earlier, some of it all the more authentic looking because it was half-eaten by moths. As she stood in front of a portrait of the saint she asked, more than half-jokingly: "If you are half as good as they say you are, find me someone to share my life with. Good man, yourself." Blessing herself in the manner she had learned from her mother more than thirty years earlier, she wondered when was she likely to make the same sign of the cross again.

Adrienne looked on as people who were crippled asked for cures, while those who thought they were past curing asked for money from passers-by. She wondered were the local social services extremely poor when so many people were begging. They were part of the European Community as much as her own country, and they must have some kind of income. Were they there because it was easier to stir hearts in such a place than anywhere else? She then thought of the many people who begged in the doorways and on bridges back home. Who was she to judge anyone? She asked herself.

There was one old woman on her knees, her body bent forward so far that her forehead touched the ground. She had one hand raised a little in which she held a plastic cup, in the hope that pilgrims who walked by would put some kind of a donation into it. It was like a throwback from some kind of Biblical story. It would take a heart of stone to refuse to put money in that cup, Adrienne thought, as she divided all the spare change she had between the various beggars. "If the only thing Anthony does is get people to put contributions into the hands of those in need," she thought, "then he and his Basilica are worth it."

She was not quite as pleased when one of the beggars followed her across the street as she tried to go to a café called Dolce Del Santo for something to eat and to get to use the toilets. The man seemed to have no legs but he was able to manouver the wheels of a pram on which he crouched with great speed. Although Adrienne had probably distributed more in charity than anyone else in the area, or perhaps he saw that she had, he targeted her and shouted out for alms as she hurried away.

Feeling a mixture of shame and anger she searched her purse again and found that all she had in cash was twenty euro which she gave to the beggar. He shouted all the louder as he chased after her in a clatter of pram wheels. She stopped in the middle of the street and roared at him to: "Fuck off." Although she did not say it in Italian, it was clear what she meant in any language. The man stopped chasing her and stared after her with a look of shock on his face. Adrienne was shaking. She thought everyone in the square was looking at her and judging her. Her legs felt weak as she almost staggered to the door of the café.

Inside she ordered a coffee and hurried into the toilets. She had never seen the likes before, a delph bowl at ground level. It was not that it was not clean but a person had to squat above it. It reminded her of stories her mother used to tell of the national school she had attended in which the toilet was a hole in a piece of timber with the excrement piled ina heap underneath. She returned to the café, paid for the coffee but left without tasting it. It may have been fine but she could not face it. She searched aroun the square until she found a hotel with the kind of toilet she was used to. It was comfortable in comparison with some of the pizzarias and trattorias she had seen in the area. She ate a plate of spaghetti with bread and butter and washed it down with a glass of wine.

"I will have to be careful," Adrienne told herself. "Wine again in the middle of the day." Looking around it seemed that is what most of the locals and tourists had with their lunches as well. "They probably have siestas," she thought. "I hope that I don't have mine on the train, or you would not know where I might end up." As far as she knew Venice was at the end of that particular train-line. She was unlikely to find herself in Rome or Naples the following morning.

Adrienne took time to recover from the ordeal she had endured when followed by the beggar on the pram-wheels. She sat for a long while sipping her chianti until she felt well enough to face the streets again. She knew her father would appreciate a present from such a shrine, so she searched until she found an icon of Jesus and Mary that was not too gaudy. "He will be delighted with that," she thought. "He will think I have gone back to the old faith, and become a disciple of Saint Anthony."

She sometimes missed the kind of certainty and consolation that faith had brought to her parent's generation, but it was something you had or didn't have. Art was her God and she recognised there was the possibility of a creator as she herself created. Did new ideas or inspiration just come from nowhere? She allowed that to remain an open question. She had strayed a long way from the traditional faith of her forbears, but she was not opposed to it like some of her secular acquaintances. "Every generation makes its own choices" was her motto.

It was obvious that religion played a big part in the lives of billions of people throughout the world. The sight of thousands of Muslim men on their knees, bowing in unison always moved her, but where were the women? As rare as in the inner sanctums of the Vatican. Religion was obviously a very powerful force too in the Southern States of the USA, with elections to the Presidency often depending on attitudes to God. It amused her to some extent to hear the name of God so frequently on the tongues of American politicians, whereas people who wore ashes on their foreheads in the Irish Dáil on Ash Wednesday were excoriated by a supposedly liberal press.

As she left the surrounds of San Antóin, Adrienne felt that this kind of devotion would continue to survive the centuries, because it answered some of people's deepest longings, in particular the desire for health in mind and body. This was a place of constant prayer, day and night. The legacy left by people like Anthony and Francis had stood the test of time. There was something less than appealing about the buying and selling of trinkets around the shrine, the beggars and the haranguers, but they were part of real life which reminded her of the way Jesus had got down and dirty to reach the poor and the needy. This, rather than the big cathedrals and the priceless paintings was what religion should be all about, or should it be about both? Adrienne let that question hang in the air.

As she returned to Venice on the train, Adrienne was thinking that she would try to get as much use as she could from that mode of transport. It was cheap and efficient. What would stop her from taking a day or overnight trip to Milan or Verona to see the galleries and do some shopping? Rome and Florence were further away but must be quite accesible on a fast train. This life in Italy was becoming more appealing by the hour. She wondered had William Shakespeare visited places such as Venice and Verona in which he had set plays, or had he just heard about them from merchants and sailors.

Adrienne did not intend to spend very much money until the settlement with Patrick was finalised. She received a certain amount each month at present and did not want to exceed that until she had an exhibition in Galway during the winter, and hopefully sold some paintings. "At good prices," she smiled to herself, and then looked around to see were other passengers laughing at this madwoman who seemed to be talking to herself. She would have to return to Ireland for the exhibition. This would give her an opportunity to visit her father and other friends, "If I have not gone mad from the lack of company in the meantime."

The nearest vaperetto stop was only a couple of hundred metres from the railway station. Adrienne was pleased to find that she was finding her way around the city much easier than on the previous day. The boat was crowded as it was around the time that many people would be returning from work. She felt scared, thinking that the boat would topple over if everyone ran to one side at the same time, but there were so many people on board that nobody could run anywhere.

Thinking of a peom by Antaine Ó Raiftéirí, "Anach Chuain" that she had learned at primary school, she thought that if this boat capsized there would be far more casualties than the "eleven men and eight women mentioned in the poem. There was no likelihood of a sheep putting its hoof through the bottom of the boat as happened at Annaghdown, but accidents happened easily. There must have been at least a hundred people on board, so Adrienne went ashore at the next stop, although she was still quite a distance from her apartment. Carrying the new shoes that were now hurting her feet, she set out to walk barefoot the rest of the way home.

There was no direct pathway along the waterside, as some buildings stood up straight from the water. Others were set back a little and had footpaths or wooden walkways to the front. The only way to go was through narrow laneways at the rear of buildings. Adrienne felt more scared there than she had been on the vapertetto, and she vowed to herself that she would take the boat, some boat, any boat all the way home anymore, that is if she got home safely.

According to her guidebook Venice was a safe city, but she had read somewhere of someone being sexually assualted or raped in one of the back lanes. Come to think of it now it was in a novel she had read that, but that did not mean that it could not happen. The next time she reached the water's edge she searched for the receipt for the fare she had paid for the water-taxi on the night she arrived in the city. She rang the mobile number and inside a few minutes the speedboat was pulling alongside. She told him her address but he said that he had not forgotten where she lived.

Adrienne asked did he keep an account of where all his clients lived, and he answered that depended on how nice and friendly they were.

"What kind of óinseach do you think I am?" she asked, inadvertently using an Irish word commonly used by English speakers to refer to someone stupid.

"You are no óinseach."

Adrienne was surprised: "You understand Gaelic?"

"Italian Gaelic," he smiled.

She tried to test him out with other questions in Gaelic, but he did not take the bait. Turning to English, she asked: "The word you used sounded very idiomatic. Where did you learn it? It was certainly not in Italy."

Giorgio shrugged his shoulders in a way he had learned from observing Italians: "You find Italians anywhere there are fish and chips. You just need to sniff out to smell the cooking oil."

"I smell nothing but the sea."

"Why did you send for me?" Giorgio asked. "Of all the water-taxis in Venice."

She answered honestly that it was the only number she could find. She told of her fear on the vaperetto because of the crowds, and her even bigger fear in the back lanes. Giorgio said the boats were very safe, but she should just ring him if she was afraid to go anywhere.

"And I'm sure I will have to pay dearly for it."

"There will be a special rate, but you may have to wait a while if I have an appointment at the airport or the hotel."

"I'll think about it," Adrienne said casually. "Anyway thank you for coming to collect me today."

"Anytime," he answered easily. "Two Irish people far from home. They should look out for each other."

Adrienne tossed back her long hair with her right hand: "So you are an Irishman now?"

"I'm a European. Like yourself."

"Where are you from?" she asked.

"Here, there and everywhere."

"You need to be more specific."

"We moved about." It was clear that Giorgio was not going to give anything away.

"Are you a long time in this city."

"Long enough."

"Talking to you is like trying to extract teeth with a pincers," was Adrienne's answer to that.

Giorgio smiled: "Keep asking and you might get to the answer."

Adrienne liked his smile: "The trouble is that I am not getting any straight answers."

"You obviously need to get to know me better."

"Why should I want to get to know someone who dodges every question? You must be a politician."

Giorgio shook his head: "A taxi driving politician, I don't think so."

The boat was now pulling into the pier beside the block which contained Adrienne's apartment. Giorgio threw a rope around the nearest pole, but he seemed to be in no hurry to finish their conversation.

"Come for dinner with me," he said, "and I guarantee that I will answer at least one of your questions."

"One question always leads to another."

"One question each evening," he smiled.

"That would cost you a bomb," Adrienne replied, "because it would mean a lot of dinners, you are so secretive."

"How do I know that you are not juat as secretive?"

"You didn't ask me any question to find out."

"I'm a man. Our species are not inquisitive."

Adrienne laughed. She did not know what to think. She had no idea what kind of a man this was, but he seemed nice. She was lonely from the lack of company. She was a free woman starting a new life. What was to lose by joining him for dinner?

She looked Giorgio straight in the eye: "Are you serious about dinner?"

"You must be hungry," was his throwaway reply.

"Do you make a joke of everything?"

"I would not have asked if I was not serious."

"When are you talking about?"

"Tonight at seven?" Giorgio said. "I have to work untiil six."

Adrienne was not too sure of herself. "I don't know. I thought that you meant at the weekend or something."

"I thought you were anxious to get answers to all yur questions." He was hard to resist.

"Where?" Adrienne asked.

"Wherever Gráinne takes us. I will be back here at seven,"

Adrienne was a bit confused: "Who is Gráinne?"

Giorgio laid his hand on the wheel of his boat: "Gráinne Mhaol, the pirate queen of Connacht."

"I don't see her name written on the boat."

"He shook his head in mock annoyance: "Questions, questions."

Adrienne stepped out on to the little pier, Giorgio loosened and freed the rope, and turned his water-taxi out into the canal. He opened the throttle and sped away, one hand on the wheel, the other waving in the air like a bad actor as he shouted: "*buona séra*" against the wind.

As Adrienne climbed the stairs to her apartment she was beginning to regret that she had accepted Giorgio's invitation to dinner. It was not that she did not feel the need for company, but she was not ready in so far as time and clothes were concerned. No way would she be ready by seven, she told herself. She was not ready in any sense of the word. She was not ready to go out with a complete stranger. What was she to do for clothes? She had not unpacked most of her luggage yet. She did not know what would be suitable to wear because she did not know what kind of place they were going to. The phrase: "up in a heap" came to her mind as a description of how she felt about this man and his invitation.

"What kind of a feather-head would accept such an invitation?" Adrienne asked herself as she entered her apartment. She decided to send a text to say that something had come up, a family emergency that would prevent her going out that night. That would buy her time to get her head together and to get proper clothes organised. Would he ever call her again if she had so obviously got cold feet? Was it not better to be out with a goodlooking man than to be looking at the walls, or at television programmes in a language that she did not understand? The same news repeated every halfhour on the only English channel she had. She wrote herself a note for the following day, to order extra TV channels and to get he laptop set up to hear news services from home.

"That is a task for tomorrow," Adrienne thought. "What am I going to do tonight?" She pulled out clothes and cast them aside. "All I have are rags." She wanted to look nice, fashionable and casual without looking 'easy.' She chose a black dress to her knees, with a small white jacket over her shoulders. She was nervous because she had not been out with any man since Patrick and herslf had split up. Would she be shy and awkward? What would they talk about? Then she thought of their conversation on the boat and how easily the banter had been between them. "It's worth a try," she told herself. If it does not work out it will hardly be news headlines tomorrow. We don't need to see each other ever again."

It was strange to meet an Irishman driving a water-taxi so far from home, but then the Irish were everywhere. "Was he married or single, separated or divorced?" was the the first question that Adrienne planned to ask Giorgio. She should have asked him already. Then she remembered that they were just going out for a meal together. It was not as if they were planning to get married and have children. "As soon as I find out that he is married," she told herself, as she peeled off the black dress and put on the red, "I will be out across that river like a seagull." She stood in front of the mirror, but thought her tummy looked too big in that. "What about the yellow one?"

viii

GIORGIO FELT A TINGLE OF excitement run through him as he prepared to go to dinner with Adrienne. It occurred to him that he did not even know her name, but how many women had he since coming to Italy whose names he could remember? This woman seemed to be different, and because of that he was prepared to take a risk. He had crossed some kind of Rubicon when the first word of Gaelic had come from his lips, and even more so when he admitted to being Irish. He was taking a chance, but hopefully it would be worth it. He felt comfortable in the presence of this woman and he enjoyed talking to her.

He had no notion of telling her anything about himself, apart from what was needed as part of a polite conversation over dinner. They might never see each other again after that nght, so there was no point in burdening anyone with information that mght be a worry to them. In some ways Giorgio felt that his choice was between living a life that gave him no real satisfaction, or trying to live as most people did, even if that was to get him into trouble. "I died officially," he told himself, "in order to stay alive, but what quality of life do I have at the moment? Whtever else you could call it, it is certainly not heaven on earth, continuously on the lookout for danger."

He found he was laughing to himself as he wondered had he fallen in love with this woman whose name he did not even know. "I'm too much of a cynic for love," he mused. Still, he had not felt like this since he had a crush on a young girl who had stayed in their house during an Irish summer course. She was tall with long blonde hair. He remembered her name alright, Muireann. He would have stood on snow to watch her on the basketball court or on the dancefloor, graceful and athletic. Some of the other girls wore miniskirts to show themselves off. It was as if Muireann was unaware of her beauty and attractiveness, not to speak of her lovely long legs. He had managed to put together a makeshift basketball ring with wire and a piece of a fishing net which he attached to the gable wall of their house. It meant that Muireann could practice her basketball skills with him in the yard while the other girls on the course painted their nails or gossipped about boys in their rooms.

It was a time of lovely innocence and unrequited love. They had great respect for eah other. Giorgio thought Muireann too beautiful to allow anything to break the magic spell between them. She knew that he had signed up to go to Rome to train to be a priest at the end of the summer. It was if they had been given those three weeks to experience an innocent and pure love, to taste a kind of mystery before real live arrived with all its burdens. They only time they had ever touched each other was accidental, as they leaped to catch the ball, or to throw it into the makeshift ring. They would be full of "Excuse me's" afterwards as if they had damaged some kind of beautiful flower, while they briefly enjoyed those seconds in which their bodies touched each other.

That taste of innocent infatuation seemed to have stirred inside Giorgio feelings of true love which he had longed for ever since but failed to find despite how many women he took to his bed, or anywhere else he had managed a quick fumble. As he shaved and showered before going out for the evening, Giorgio felt that he would love to rekindle that kind of long lost love with this new woman he had recently met. "Am I out of my mind?" he asked his image in the mirror. "Always the idealist, always the eejit. The fool who ran after the moon and ended up lying in the gutter." It was the same kind of idealism which had led him to kill, to leave children orphans, wives widows. All for what? So that old enemies would end up drinking tea together in Stormont Castle, with the likes of him abandoned and dumped on the dungheap of history.

"People suffered on both sides of the conflict," Giorgio told himself, "some worse than others." People who had gained from the peace process, suffered, as did those who had gained nothing. It had all been predicted by the great socialist, James Connolly back before 1916. What was the point in changing the colour of the flag that flew above Government buildings, or changing the badges on soldier's caps if the poor remained poor after the revolution? What have the people of the Falls or the Shankill gained from the Troubles? Broken hearts and gravestones, with sectarianism probably worse that it had ever been.

Giorgio felt that the real reason for the success of the peace process had been tiredness. Credit was given to politicians inside and outside the State, but the most important thing that had happened was that people just grew tired of conflict. There was no longer any heart for the fight. People wanted a normal life, just as he did at present. A life without having to constantly look over your shoulder. Peace. He imagined himself being interviewed on television about what was the ultimate result of idealism. He would knock the wind from the interviewers sails with his answer: "People just get tired."

That is why revolutions are always doomed to failure, Giorgio thought. Even Alexander the Great ran out of road. He became frustrated when there were no more worlds to conquer, but at least he had reached his goals while still a young man. As for the great revolutionaries of the previous hundred years, men like Lenin, Trotsky and Stalin basically ran out of ideas as well as of idealism. They achieved their goals too easily, and finding blood so easy to shed, they continued to do so even when it was getting them nowhere. They had never really thought out what to do next once the old powerhouse was toppled.

"What kind of fool am I?" Giorgio wondered, "Flying off on tangents while I prepare to have dinner with a beautiful woman." He intended to be on his very best behaviour, courteous, kind, thoughtful, the perfect gentleman whose only task was to ensure that his dinner companion enjoyed the evening. At this moment that was all he desired. Good company, friendship, conversation. If anything else was to come of their getting together, he would certainly welcome that. Right now it was just a possible consequence. He could take it or leave it. He had grown tired of fleeting physical one night stands.

He had no idea of what he was going to tell this woman about himself or his life. Those answers would come to him when they were needed. He intended to talk about her and her life. He had rarely met anyone who did not enjoy talking about themselves. That was not just cynicism. It was the most natural thing in the world. People knew more about themselves, their history, hopes and dreams than they knew about anything else. He felt there was little point in planning for the night ahead. It was likely to turn out differently from anything he was likely to imagine.

ix

GIORGIO WAS QUITE SATISFIED WITH himself when he had dressed up in what he considered his best clothes. These had a cowboy feel to them, with high boots and a leather hat. The hat was a mild form of disguise as it hid the eyes when tipped forward. He felt slightly awkward in the high boots but began to get a feel for them when he went downstairs and outside to where his boat was tied. He headed in the direction of the apartment to which he had delivered the young Irish woman some evenings earlier. He hooted his foghorn a couple of times, not just because there were a couple of gondolas in the middle of the canal, but because he was feeling better than he had felt in a long time. He thought he must be like a teenager on his first date, full of nerves as well as joy and hope.

When he reached his destination, Giorgio tied his boat in the usual casual manner he used when he was not staying long in a particular place. Time seemed to drag as he waited. "Is she going to leave me here like a stupid fool?" he asked himself when there was no sign of his date. He looked at his watch and realised that he was actually ten mintes before the time arranged. He sat into the boat and switched on the radio to let an operatic aria pass the time.

Adrienne arrived unknown to him: "Music and all," she said. "Isn't this romantic?"

Giorgio jumped out of the boat and took her hand to help her into his water-taxi.

Adrienne told him: "I'm alright. Steady on there. This dress was not made for swimming, but thank you for being so courteous."

"I can't afford to let you take a tumble in the cabin like the last time," Giorgio said.

"Do you ever forget anything?"

"You are looking lovely. One thing I didn't forget was how nice you looked, even nicer when you are all dressed up."

"I must have looked terrible the last day in my old rags," was Adrienne's reply.

Giorgio answered with a version of an old Gaelic proverb: "It is not the silk suit that counts, but the person that wears it."

"Are you calling me a goat?" asked Adrienne micchieviously.

"What would make you think that?"

"I know the correct version of that proverb—'Even if you put a silk suit on a goat, it is still a goat."

Giorgio shook his head: "A man can't win that kind of an argument. You certainly do not look anything like a goat."

"So says the old puck of a cowboy." Adrienne did not know where the talk was coming from, but it covered up her nervousness. Anything was better than silence in such circumstances, she thought.

Giorgio freed the rope and turned his boat out towards the centre of the canal: "it is you that is doing the name-calling now," he said lightly.

"Where are we going?" Adrienne asked as the boat gained speed.

"The Trattoria La Campana. The food is tasty and there are nice paintings on the walls."

"You can't eat paintings," Adrienne shouted above the noise of the engine, anything to keep the talk going.

"I thought it was a place that would suit a painter," he said. "Or should I say an artist?"

"I never said that I am an artist."

"I saw the stuff you had with you the first day," was Giorgio's answer to that. "I am not as stupid as I look."

"You know what curiosity did to the cat?"

"The things were very obvious. I couldn't miss them."

"Maybe they were not mine," said Adrienne.

"I didn't notice anyone else."

Adrienne laughed: "You will get a job as a detective if the tourism industry ever fails. It would suit you. You have that Crocodile Dundee look in that hat."

"Tourism is one industry that will never fail here. There will be people coming to this city until she sinks beneath the waves."

"And you will still have your little boat to escape in. Do you really think that it is going to sink?"

Giorgio shrugged: "So they say, but it is unlikely to happen until we have finished our dinner this evening." He pulled into a small pier from which a narrow lane led across to the commercial area.

"Will the boat be safe here?" Adrienne asked as he tied it securely.

"It hasn't been stolen so far. This city actually has a good reputation in that regard." Giorgio reached for her hand. "Let's go. Don't worry about the boat."

They reached a street full of shops and cafes, with some outdoor stalls in alcoves and small squares. There were masks of all shapes, sizes and designs for sale everywhere, some of them extremely ornate.

"Would you like me to get you one?" Giorgio asked.

Adrienne shrugged her shoulders as if to say she didn't mind either way: "We are a long way from Halloween."

"They are not confined to that time of the year around here. There are major parades with the streets full of people, everyone wearing a mask. It is really colourful."

"I don't like them very much," Adrienne replied. "A lot of them are beautifully made and very artistic, but one of them would scare me if I saw it in the middle of the night."

"You could see worse."

"You are not that bad," She pushed him playfully.

Giorgio took he hand and led Adrienne through crowds of people. They seemed to be from every nation on earth. Some carried luggage. Others rolled suitcases behind them along the cobbled streets. Everywhere there seemed to be tourists searching for the accomodation they had booked. They had no means of transport in that part of the city other than their legs.

Adrienne and Giorgio came to a square with a large church in one corner, and shops, cafes and people begging all over the place.

"There are good pictures in that church," Giorgio said. "From the sixteenth century. They are well worth seeing."

"You seem to have art on the brain," was Adrienne's reaction. "I have more than one interest in life. I thought we were going out to eat tonight."

"I was only saying," Giorgio answered. "I just thought that you might be interested."

"Whatever you say yourself. Food today. Art tomorrow."

"We are not far from that trattoria now." Giorgio led Adrienne through the crowds to a narrow street at the corner of the square. About a hundred metres further they reached the place he intended that they would eat. His choice surprised Adrienne but she did not say anything in case he was short of money. She expected something more elaborate for their first date. When he chose the house wine she was convinced that money was scarce, but her reservations went out the window when she tasted the wine and the food arrived quicker than any other food outlet she had visited so far.

"That spaghetti is wonderful," she said admiringly. "Do they make it themselves."

"It's all down to a secret recipe," Giorgio replied. "It's the way that they squeeze the pasta between their toes in the bath as they pull up on the strings." He leant back as if giving a demonstration.

Adrienne laughed heartily: "Really, though. Is it made in-house?"

"I just eat it. I don't ask questions." Giorgio spoke as best he could while trying to direct stray strings into his mouth. "It is certainly worth coming herr for the spaghetti alone."

Adrienne sat back in her chair when she finished the first course. The plate was taken away by a middleaged woman who seemed to be stressed and overworked. A male cook of somewhat the same age came from the kitchen and went to the front door to smoke a cigarette. The woman addressed him in a loud and angry voice and before long he was shouting back. Giorgio seemed impervious to it all. Adrienne had to cover her mouth to hold back her laughter.

Giorgio looked at her and asked: "What is it?"

"I never heard the likes of it in a public place."

"I thought you were about to get sick or something," Giorgio said, "when I saw you with your hand to your mouth."

"Wouldn't it be great to understand what they are saying?"

"That kind of an argument is the same in any language. People here don't seem to mind who is listening."

Adrienne said that it would make a wonderful drama.

"There you are. It's all free. You would have to pay to see that at home in the Abbey Theatre."

"She must be good at her work," Adrienne observed.

"What makes you think that?"

"If she wasn't, she would surely get the sack for attacking your man like that. She went through him for a shortcut."

Giorgio laughed: "It's her husband. They are not so easy to get rid of, especially in Italy. Anyway they are probably madly in love despite all that."

"They are certainly passionate when it comes to fighting."

"You would forgive them anything," Giorgio said, "when they put food like that on the table."

The family row rumbled on but the courses kept coming. Adrienne concentrated on her food to prevent herself laughing at the absurdity of it all from her point of view. Giorgio ate his veal without any comment, while she had prawns. It was he who broke the silence when it was becoming slightly uncomfortable:

"You didn't say what you think of the pictures?" He indicated the paintings that hang on the walls of the trattoria.

Adrienne, who had a quick look at them on her way in, gave them a little more attention. They were mainly of bridges and gondolas as well as some of the historic buildings of Venice. The idea that pleased her most was that you could display and sell pictures in such a place.

"They are nice enough," she replied. "I'm sure that the tourists love them. They reflect the city and make good presents. They remind people of their holidays, I suppose, like good photographs or postcards."

"But they are not art?" Giorgio asked. "They are alright for the ordinary person, but they wouldn't be good enough for someone who really appreciates art."

Adrienne smiled: "It is you that said it. Are you calling me a snob now?"

"It is you who said it," he replied with a laugh.

Adrienne held her head to one side in a way that appealed to Giorgio, as she studied the pictures again: "Some of them actually are good," she said. "Do you see that one with the city covered in snow. Technically that is very well done. That is the one that really stands out. All of the others are too similar to each other."

"They might all be by the same painter," was Giorgio's opinion.

"Are they all signed by the same person?" Adrienne asked. "I can't see properly without my reading glasses."

Giorgio turned around in his chair to check, but turned back immediately to his meal

"That wasn't much of a look," Adrienne said.

"I thought your man with the beard sitting beneath the picture thought that I was staring at him."

"Don't be daft. The pictures are there to be looked at. I'm sure he realises that is what you were doing."

"I saw enough," Giorgio answered. He had got somewhat of a shock when he thought he recognised the man sitting below the picture. He was older and heavier than Giorgio remembered. His hair was longer and he had a beard, but he was sure that he met him in Long Kesh prison many years earlier. He had never been a prisoner himself, but had gone there, supposedly as a relative of one of the prisones, but really as part of a delegation seeking prisoner's views on a possible ceasefire.

Giorgio was now on full alert, and did not realise that Adrienne was talking to him: "I never actually had you down as being shy."

"Is he still looking at me?" he asked.

"Paranoid as well," she said.

Giorgio tried to compose himself: "You know yourself that it is not good manners to stare someone in the face, especially when they are eating."

At the same time he was debating with himself whether to cut and run, or just wait there and act as if nothing was wrong. The man beneath the picture had given no indication that he had recognised him. He decided to sit it out for a while, cut short the meal and leave with his date like any normal couple.

Adrienne was still talking about the picture: "He would know well that you were looking at the painting, not at him."

"Forget about the bloody picture," Giorgio said roughly: "Is he watching me?" he asked.

Adrienne frowned: "Is who watching you?"

"Your man under the picture."

"Are you losing it or something?"

Giorgio asked crossly: "Is he looking at me, or what is he doing?"

"He is just eating his dinner like a normal person."

"Come on," Giorgio said, as he stood up from the table.

"What's your hurry? I was looking forward to one of those desserts."

"Are you coming or staying?" Giorgio asked in a loud whisper which conveyed the message that he certainly was not staying.

Adrienne stood up. Giorgio grabbed her hand before she had time to put on her coat. He grabbed that and threw it across his arm, threw money on the table and headed for the door. Fifty metres or so away he pulled Adrienne into the darkness of a doorway and signelled her to stay quiet. He kept a close eye on the door of the trattoria for a couple of minutes to check if they were being followed. Letting go of Adrienne's arm, he said:

"I think that it's alright now."

"What is alright?" she asked: "Do you owe money to that man or what?"

"I will explain it again," he said. "It has nothing to do with crime. Not on my side anyway. It's just that I am working undercover, if you understand what I am saying."

"For the cairbineri?" Adrienne asked.

Giorgio continued to lie: "Higher up again. For the Government."

"You are a spy?"

"I think you may have watched too many James Bond films."

"Are you with Interpol or what? she asked"

"It's lower key than that. It's part of the lookout for the kind of terrorist that bombed Madrid and Turkey. Eyes and ears." he said conspiratorially.

"What have I let myself in for? Adrienne wondered aloud.

Giorgio put a finger to his lips as if he could not reveal anything else. He did not want to tell any more lies until he had time to think. At least he had turned her attention from his rudeness in the trattoria.

"Would you mind staying for a while in the hotel down the street?" he asked, "until I check this fellow out properly." He grabbed Adrienne's hand before she had time to reply and led her down a street of shops and restaurants until they reached Hotel Principe. "You will be safe here until I get back," he said when they reached the hotel bar. "I have a tab here so you can order any kind of drink you like. Johnny will look after you. Don't worry, I won't be long."

"I'd prefer to go back to my apartment," Adrienne said, worriedly. "I don't like any of this stupid carry-on."

Giorgio spoke sternly: "There is nothing stupid about a matter of life or death. I have to hurry or that fellow will have disappeared." He took money from his pocket and placed it on a table. "That will get you a water-taxi if you want to go home immediately."

"Go on," she said. "I'll wait." He was going out the door by the time she said: "Be careful."

Adrienne flopped down in an armchair as if all her energy had suddenly drained from her body. She had certainly never expected anything like this when she agreed to go out for dinner. She regretted at the same time that she had not told him to be careful while he was still in earshot. What if he was to be killed out there without having heard a kind word from her?"

Giorgio made his way back to the trattoria, turning around suddenly from time to time to check if he was being followed. He stopped beside the window and checked the movements of passers-by before turning to look inside. The man who had worried him was sitting opposite a younger woman, his hand on hers. From his sideface view this probably was not the man Giorgio had suspected earlier, but he felt that he could not be too careful. He needed to know, to take evasive or other action if it was required.

He waited outside until the couple finished their meal and emerged from the trattoria. He followed in the hope of hearing their accents. American, he thought, but that could be a cover. He tapped the man on the shoulder and asked for directions to the railway station. He realised from their face to face contact that this was a case of mistaken identity. He had over-reacted and had probably lost any chance of another date with the young Irishwoman he had brought to dinner.

Adrienne stood up the minute he entered the bar of the Principe and said that she wanted to go back to her apartment immediately.

"Will you not wait for one drink? My friend Johnny here makes cocktails to die for."

"I've had enough for one night," she said in a serious voice. "I'll order another taxi if you can't take me." She headed for the door.

"There is no need to go overboard about it," Giorgio said. "I'll take you. It's the least I can do."

Adrienne did not speak during the water-taxi journey, and apart from a curt word of thanks as she alighted from the boat, she kept her own counsel.

X

ADRIENNE BARELY SLEPT THE NIGHT she had been out with Giorgio. Tossing and turning in her bed, she tried to make sense or reason from what had happened. She was sure of one thing. She had no intention of going anywhere with that fellow again. He was too much trouble. She had come to ths place in search of quietness and contentment, and all she had found from the first man she had met was conspiracy and spying. If that was the kind of life she had wanted, she told herself, she would have joined the *French Foreign Legion*, or some crowd like that. "I doubt if they accept women," she thought, "but that doesn't matter. I won't be joining any organisation." The last thing in the world she would want was to have anything to do with violence or militarism.

It was at times like this that Adrienne missed Patrick, her former husband. Whatever else you could say about him, he was steady and solid, the kind of man who would never get involved in any kind of political or social unrest. His colleagues from work, or those he would bring home to dinner were hewn from the same kind of rock. There would be no revolutions on their watch. That was only one side of Patrick, of course, as she had found out the hard way. The seemingly quiet sensible type was having an affair with a woman in the office. They were expecting a child. Could any man be trusted? Could any person be trusted? In spite of everything she felt like calling Patrick, just to hear his voice. She checked her watch and realised that it was the middle of the night in Dublin as well.

Adrienne imagined Patrick waking up and reaching for the phone, wondering who could be calling at this time of the night. Sheila would be stirring by his side, asking what was wrong, who was that on the phone. Then the row would start. Why was Adrienne ringing? Was his marriage over or not? It was not as if they had children and one of them was sick. But calling because she was lonely, or because she had a bad date. "She should get over it," would be Sheila's reaction. "That woman is still in love with you. That or she isn't well in the head."

"Do I still love him?" Adrienne asked herself as she got out of bed and went to make a cup of tea. Coffee would keep her from sleep, not that it mattered much as she was unlikely to sleep that night anyway. She missed hot chocolate as she would have had at home, but she had not seen it for sale in the supermarkets. When she had made tea she answered her own question: "No, I do not love Patrick any more. Not after the way he betrayed me. I could never go back to him. That is not to say that I do not miss the companionship, someone to share thoughts with, someone to just talk to about even the most trivial things.

Earlier in the evening she had a vague hope of developing such a relationship with the water-taxi driver, but she knew now that there was more to his life than bringing people to and from the airport and other destinations. Adrienne knew that there were people who enjoyed that kind of life, who loved danger, the type of a man who smelt of dynamite. "If I was fifteen years younger," she mused, "but not now. What I want now is peace and contentment. If that exists."

Adrienne returned to bed when she finished her tea, but soon realised that she was wasting her time trying to get to sleep. She got up and wrapped her dressinggown around her. She stood out on the balcony and waited for the sun to rise. The soft glow of colour on the horizon heralded the peeping disc that seemed to break the surface, delay for a while as if checking that it was alright to appear, and then emerge as a golden ball at the bottom of the sky, with an aura of rich colour all around it.

Adrienne returned quickly to the inside of the apartment to collect a sketchbook and some handpaints. She made one sketch after another, as the colours of the rising and risen sun changed. She knew at that moment that she would work on those images later with oil on canvas. She was working again. She was back in the artistic saddle. That was the moment that she knew that the weight of the world had lifted from her shoulders. Her marriage was over, her new life had begun. Events of the previous night didn't matter any more. "To hell with the lot of them."

She decided to call her father. He was the only man she felt she could rely on. A woman with an English accent answered the phone. Adrienne had forgotten the name of the woman her father had mentioned in their last conversation.

"Are you lving there now?" She knew as soon as the words left her tongue that she had failed to conceal her surprise.

The woman at the other end of the phone burst out laughing: "I'm just the home help. I come in for a couple of hours twice a week. There is no need to get jealous of me, love."

Adrienne wanted to tell her that she was not her love. Instead she asked: "What do you mean jealous?"

"I thought you might be one of his women friends."

Adrienne was getting even more surprised: "He has more than one?"

"Can I tell him who is calling, love?"

"His daughter. Adrienne, ringing from Italy."

"Sorry love, I didn't know. Wait until I bring the phone into the bedroom. He likes to leave it in the kitchen at night in case of radiation."

"Thank you," Adrienne said when what she really wanted to say was that she knew her father and his likes and dislikes.

Her father enjoyed the idea that he might have a woman staying with him. "I'm glad it's not this one anyway," he said in Gaelic. She might qualify as one of the ugly sisters in Cinderella."

"What a thing to say," his daughter tut-tutted, while giggling at the same time. "I hope she is not listening to you."

"She hasn't a word of Irish, and not too much English either."

"Not very politically correct, Dad."

"Are you going to report me to the PC police?"

"I'll think about it," Adrienne answered lightly.

"You are still lonely out there?" her father asked.

"What makes you think that?"

"Because you are calling so often and so early."

Adrienne put the question: "Would you prefer if I didn't?"

"Feel free to ring as often as you like," her father told her. "Remember the phones are dear in other countries."

"Yes Dad, I know," she said with a slight sarcasm. "And they cause radiation, and burn the hairs in your ears."

"Mock away, but wait until you get your bill."

"Calls from here are not very dear at this time of the day," she answered, although she did not really know anything about them. "But if I am disturbing youself and your women."

I have only one woman at this time of the day, the woman you spoke to already." Her father was pleased to hear that she had begun to paint again, even if was only preliminary sketches. Adrienne waxed lyrical about the sunrise, and invited him to visit as soon as he could.

"As long as you don't expect me to greet the sunrise," he joked.

When their conversation ended Adrienne mused about how perceptive her father had been about her loneliness. He would probably come to visit sooner than expected because of that. She called Patrick next, in his office, so that she would not have to speak to Sheila. Although she worked in the same place, Adrienne guessed that she would be on maternity leave at this stage.

"Is there something wrong? was her former husband's reaction to her phonecall.

"I just wanted to find out how you are."

"You never asked that before."

"I'm asking it now. I just wanted to let you know that I have arrived in Venice and that the apartment is fine."

"Good for you," he said coldly.

Adrienne told herself not to react. "Would you like my address and phone number?"

"Why would I need them?"

"There are still legal issues to be ironed out."

"I can't afford any more money," he said.

"I'm not asking for money. Anyway I'm painting again, and I expect to ba able to look after myself."

"Aren't you to have an exhibition in Galway sometime?" Patrick asked vaguely of the woman to whom he had been married for years. It sounded as if he was just making conversation.

"Nothing has been arranged yet," she answered lightly. "I just wanted to let you know how things are." She hesitated, before adding: "We were together a long time. We had some good times, and they will never be forgotten by me anyway."

It was as if Patrick suddenly became animated: "We could have those good times again."

"You know it's over, Patrick?"

"We could have sorted something out if you were not in such a hurry to leave me."

"It was not me that was unfaithful," Adrienne said, as gently as she could.

"Have you never heard of forgiveness?" he asked. "Not to speak of till death do us part."

"A pity you didn't remember those vows before pulling down your trousers," Adrienne answered.

Patrick let out a sigh but did not reply. It was as if he wanted to hang up the phone but was too mannerly to do so.

"How is Sheila?" Adrienne asked, as if making the point to Patrick that their own relationship was over.

"I'm sure you care."

"It wasn't easy to ask since she is expecting your baby, but I don't wish any harm to the child."

"Only to its parents," was Patrick's surly reply.

"If you want to be childish, carry on like that. It might be time to grow up now that you are going to be a father."

Patrick got the message: "She is as good as can be expected."

"She has not long to go now?" Adrienne mused.

"Not long." It was as if he could not wait to hang up.

"I hope everything goes alright." Adrienne found that difficult to say in the circumstances, but she did not want their conversation to end with them fighting: "By the way do you know yet if is a boy or a girl?"

Patrick cut across her question: "Sorry, but I have to deal with an important item here. Excuse me, please. I'll be talking to you one of the days."

Adrienne wondered was Sheila still working, and had come into his office. Why should that surprise her? Wasn't that how it had all started? On the desk, probably. She tried to drive that image from her mind. Maybe she should give Patrick some credit. She had never thought much of his job, probably had not shown enough respect for what he did. Perhaps he really did have to deal with something serious. Still she was disappointed. Talking to him was like talking to a stranger. She wondered why had she called him at all. "I will have to find a way to deal with my loneliness," she told herself. She decided to arrange Italian classes immediately. That and the painting should be enough to keep her mind occupied

xi

GIORGIO WENT ABOUT HIS WORK with a little more energy the following day. He had slept well. He had some regrets that things had not worked out better with Adrienne, but he had found out at least that the man in the trattoria was not one of those out to get him. There would be other women. There always were, but then this one may not have been completely lost to him. If he got another chance he would take her to the Principe. He knew the staff and he was less likely to have someone from the past creep up on him unawares there. He had wondered for a while the previous night would he need to kill the fellow in the restaurant. He would have if the man had recognised him. It was the law of the jungle, kill or be killed. There was little choice. It would just have been self-defence.

He hoped that he would never have to kill anyone again. He would only do so if his life was in danger. History still hung over him and his kind. There was a kind of peace but there were still unresolved issues, loose ends to be tied up. It was easy enough to kill someone, but there were practical difficulties hiding or disposing of a corpse. He had plans for such a circumstance. He had his boat and there was plenty of deep water out the bay. A couple of concrete blocks would see to it that a person would never be found.

Giorgio had learned enough down through the years to ensure that no trace of DNA or other evidence would be left behind. He had often thought while on training courses with the volunteers that too much time was spent explaining and teaching people how to clean up crime scenes properly. He understood the reasons better now. How many of his comrades were free to walk the streets because they had not left that kind of evidence after them while in military action for their country.

The bitter truth for Giorgio was that most of his former comrades were becouse of the Anglo-Irish accord known as the Good Friday agreement. Many of them were now parliamentarians with a good income and a high profile. Why had nobody thought of those in his position when those arrangements were being made? The leadership had battled hard for the freedom of those who had killed a detective in Limerick, but had not moved a finger to help those whose deaths had been faked. It would have been too much of an embarrassment to admit their existence. The only other explanation was that they were an insurance policy in case the peace process did not work out.

It would not have been difficult to admit their existence, that their deaths were faked as part of the war, just as British agents had gone underground in more senses than one during the same period. They should have got the same treatment as those who were on the run in Britain, Australia, the United States or Canada and who were now free to return and settle at home anytime they wanted. All Giorgio or anyone else wanted now was to go back to see their own people and their own place now and again. They did not want to unsettle any applecarts.

Such thoughts were put aside as Giorgio went about his work. He had a call to the airport to take a group of Japanese tourists to the Guggenheim gallery and have them back again for a flight later in the evening. They paid well to keep himself and his taxi idle outside the gallery and then outside a hotel diningroom while they were eating. It meant that he could not do any other business in between, but that was the kind of day he liked. It gave him time to relax and read, or just to wash or polish up his water-taxi.

The speed and the hurry of some tourists was a perpetual source of surprise to Giorgio. They were not just flitting from one city to another like some visitors, but flying from one country to another as if they needed to see the whole world in a fortnight. So much for 'around the world in eighty days.' It was closer to eighty hours for some of them. "They would see more on the television at home than they get to see on their hectic journeys," he told himself. Still, he was not complaining. He was milking the money cow and she was giving her milk in abundance.

Giorgio got into a conversation with a young woman who was holding on to the rail to the right of his steering. She had broken English, but enough to keep up a kind of conversation. He learned that she had two weeks free in the year from her job in the stockmarket, and she wanted to see the whole world in that time.

"You will see everything, and you will see nothing," he told her. He had to repeat that statement in a couple of different ways before she grasped what he meant.

"I would like more time," she explained. "I have to take life as he comes." She waved her hand towards the city: "I see this. That enough today."

Giorgio agreed with her, and then said the first thing that came into his head, the kind of thing he said to most girls he met in the course of his work, "You could stay a few days with me, and I would show you the city."

"Why do I do that?" was her reply. "I here today. Paris tomorrow. New York next day. Good life."

"You will be worn out," Giorgio said. "Stay with me and you will see one city well."

The woman laughed: "Mans all same," she said, "Japan, Italy, America. One thing on mind."

"Life has to be enjoyed," Giorgio said. "We only have one life, so we need to make the best of it."

"I enjoy." She waved her hand again towards the city. "I like life. See the world."

"You are young and beautiful. You are in the city of romance. You can be as alive as you want to be."

"You not happy?" she asked Giorgio.

"Do I look as if I am not happy?"

"I happy too. I see the world. I have good job. I happy."

"In a boring job in finance?" Giorgio tried to get a reaction other than 'I happy."

She pointed to her head: "Job make me think."

Giorgio had to concentrate then on the boat traffic in the central canal. He told the woman he woulfd like to talk to her on the way back to the airport. She smiled from ear to ear, but he suspected she did not understand what he was saying. He knew that she had no notion of staying, but their chat would shorten the journey. The area close to the Guggenheim was very busy as buses had arrived from the hotels around Lake Garda with tourists who seemed to have booked every single gondola in Venice for their photo opportunities.

Tying his water-taxi to a pole as near to the gallery as he was able, Giorgio arranged to meet the Japanese group in exactly an hour. This gave him time to walk around the area. He bought a slice of pizza from a window that opened onto a sidestreet. He liked those places because the pizza was usually authentic in that it was prepared on the premesis rather than the base being taken from the freezer to be coated and placed in the oven.

The Japanese girl who had spoken to him on their journry from the airport was first back to the boat. She sat beside him on top of the little cabin as if they had known each other all their lives.

"Did you like Picasso?" he asked. He had not been inside the gallery but he was aware that the artist with the bestknown name was the one who drew most tourists to the gallery. He thought the girl beside him looked as a girl who had seen the Blessed Virgin in Lourdes might look. She shook her head slowly from side to side in awe and wonder.

"The most nice thing I ever see," she replied.

"What about the other pictures?" She did not seem to recognise the cynicism in his voice. As far as he was concerned it was the big name that atracted attention rather than the quality of the work.

She shook her head again: "Picasso alive." He lost her in her attempt to explain what the original meant to her."

"Dou you like the picture because it's good or because Picasso painted it.?" Giorgio asked.

"Good, good," she said before breaking into Japanese in her effort to communicate.

"Many people I bring here do not like it," Giorgio said.

"You see?" She pointed in the direction of the gallery,

He lied: "Very often. Too often."

"You not like?"

He shook his head slowly. "I've seen a lot better in a children's classroom."

The young woman did not seem to understand what he meant, but knew that he was disparaging Picasso.

"You know nothing," she said.

"You look lovely when you are wound up."

"I not understand."

"You should get vexed more often. It suits you," Giorgio smiled. "You should go to see Picasso more often. It brings out the passion in you. I wonder is the great painter aware of the way he effects women even when he is dead."

The Japanese woman looked at him as if she didn't know what to make of him. At that moment he would have loved to have kissed her and forgotten for a while about Adrienne and all the other women he had ever met.

The other members of the party were returning. There was work to be done. He helped a couple of older ones onto the boat as he prepared to bring them to a hotel for the meal they had booked. Later as they headed back towards the airport the young woman stood beside him again. They talked as best they could, given her difficulties with the language. It was just a polite passing of the time. Giorgio felt that they were like ships passing each other in the night. They would never meet again.

xii

ADRIENNE STOOD BACK FROM HER canvas. She was nervous and excited, alive with adrenalin, her first picture painted in almost a year. There were newspapers strewn all around the floor to protect the varnished boards. She had a sheet thrown across the table. There were tubes of paint all over the place. She knew that she needed a studio, but this would do for the present. At that moment all she cared about was that she was working again. It was not that she had ever really given up. She had drifted. After having her previous paintings framed for an exhibition she had taken time out to come to terms with the break-up of her marriage. She had just put getting back to work on the long finger, and after a while it had begun to look impossible.

She had thrown herself into her painting for a while after separating from Patrick, but as soon as she had enough for the exhibition she felt that she needed a rest. Looking back now she knew that she had been depressed. Getting back to work now felt like a life after death. She felt like changing some of the colours because the picture had come too easily to her. At the same time she was aware that change was unlikely to improve what she had done, but the opposite. It was a case of leaving very well done alone.

Adrienne sat in front of her picture, a cup of coffee in her right hand. She felt that a mother of a newborn must feel something like this, She had never had that experience, but felt that creativity must give some taste of what it meant to bring new life into the world. Soon enough Patrick and Sheila would have such feelings, while she could only imagine them. On this day she was not going to allow them or anyone else to bring her down into the dark morass in which she had existed during those times she was unable to work. She was back in business and all she wanted was to begin her next picture. She did not allow herself to do so. She mght just make a mess of it in her eagarness to do too much.

This had been a temptation right through her life. She never wanted to stop when things were going well for her, whether that was riding a horse, playing the piano or painting a picture. The trouble was that when she did stop she found it hard to begin again without pressure from her mother or father. She smiled to herself at the thought of her mother reining her in so that she would not do too much this time and then become tired from the effort. Adrienne went out on her balcony for a minute and returned again to look at her picture from a different perspective. There was no obvious connection between what she had seen outside and the abstract picture on the canvas, but she felt she had captured the essence of Venice in some way.

Although she had bought a piece of fresh cod which she intended to cook for her evening meal, Adrienne decided to eat out instead to reward herself for a good day's work. She felt also that she needed to escape the smell of the oil-paint. She had noticed a little café nearby with tables and chairs on the street outside, It seemed as if it was frequented by local people and had nice simple home-cooked food. She ordered gnocchi, because she did not recognise some of the foods which were written in Italian only on the menu. The waiter seemed to be proprieter and cook as well, and it was clear that he had little English. He was kind and gave her a couple of samples of housewine to taste before deciding which to drink. She then sat quietly while her meal was being prepared, and watched the world pass by.

Adrienne felt as if the world was going on around her and she was just there as an invisible observer. There were children on their way home from school, people returning from work, tourists reading their maps or taking pictures on their digital cameras. She remembered how she had sometimes felt in her youth, that she was the only person living in the world, that all other people were really actors pretending that thay were real people, but they were just there to observe or to try her out to see would she make mistakes.

In more innocent times she had imagined that everyone was some kind of angel, good or bad, sent by God to test her in one imaginary situation or another. Right now she felt the complete opposite to that, that she was not there at all except as an observer as everyone else got on with life as if she did not exist. "But I am alive," she told herself, "more alive than I have been for a long time, because I am back at work again."

She only realised how hungry she was when the food arrived. She ate the first course quickly and took it easy with the second which consisted of an amalgam of shellfish. She found it strange the way courses were served, with meat or fish coming separately from vegetables or pasta in many cases. "When in Rome," she told herself, or at least "when in Venice . . ." Adrienne took her time with the rest of the meal, sipping her wine and picking at the mussel shells as long as any taste of fish or sauce remained on them. The waiter hovered around her in an agitated manner, as if he was ready to take the chair from benrath her, as all the others were occupied at this stage. A queue of customers bagan to form, waiting for empty spaces. She had always heard that a queue was a great sign of a restaurant or café, but in this case it was putting pressure on her. The more the waiter hovered around, the more she wanted to dig in her heels and enjoy what was left of her wine.

The owner/waiter/chef sighed loudly when Adrienne took a notebook from her handbag and began to sketch the street and the lengthening line of people waiting to find places to sit at table. He waved a finger at her: "No picture. Private." He continued with a stream of Italian which was so fast that she did not understand any of it. She guessed that it was less than complimentary from the way that people looked at her. Knowing it was time to leave, she splashed the last of her wine on the cobbles as if there was dirt in the glass. Slowly she stood up, arranged her jacket on her shoulders and walked back to her apartment. Filling a glass of wine from a bottle she had opened the previous evening, she stood out on the balcony in the balmy air of the evening.

At that moment Adrienne decided what picture she would paint next. Here was an opportunity to sketch the rising and the setting of the sun in the same day. She went inside, left her glass of wine on the table, took her sketchbook and paint-pencils and returned to the balcony. Working at great speed she moved from page to page to grasp the different moods of the sun as the sky darkened and the colours changed. Aware that the sketches would not be wonderful after a few glasses of wine, she worked even faster. It was not technical excellence that she sought but the atmosphere of Venice during a sunset. She promised herself that she would begin on her new canvas as soon as she awoke the following day.

It came almost as a shock to hear her mobile phone ring. Her first reaction was to wonder what was wrong. Very few people knew her number. The phone was inside the apartment and although it continued to ring she could not find where exactly it was. The ringing stopped as she dumped the contents of her handbag on the table, but she still could not find it. When it began to ring again she remembered that she had put it in a cardigan pocket. She managed to press the button before the ninth and final ring.

"It's Sheila," Patrick said. "They had to take her in."

"Take her in where?" To Adrienne it sounded as if she had to be taken away for psychiatric reasons.

"To the maternity, of course," was Patrick's surly reply.

"Had she a bad turn?"

"You could say that."

"I'm sorry to hear it. What exactly is wrong?"

"The doctors are keeping her monitored. That is all that they are saying," he answered.

"So she has not lost the baby or anything?"

"She had a bad pain."

Adrienne tried to reassure him: "No matter what they say the health system is better than ever, especially in the maternity departments."

"People often come out of hospital worse than they went in," was Patrick's opinion. "That MRSA is the devil altogether."

"I've never heard of anyone having that in a maternity hospital." Adrienne tried to reassure her former husband even though she knew well that the fact that she had not heard about it did not mean that it never happened.

It was clear from Patrick's tone that he was fearing the worst: "I knew I'd be cursed for what I did."

"I certainly didn't curse you," Adrienne told him. "Anyway I don't believe in that kind of thing. I wouldn't wish any harm on a child especially."

"It's me that's responsible for it all," Patrick insisted. "I made a mess of everything, and now the little baby as to suffer for it."

Adrienne was getting impatient with him: "That has nothing to do with whatever is wrong tonight. Sometimes things go wrong with a pregnancy and it's nobody's fault."

"I miss you so much," Patrick said.

"Are you drunk or what?" Adrienne asked.

"I had a few drinks when they sent me home from the hospital. They said there was no point in me waiting. Sheila needed to sleep and there was no need to stay. They would send for me if I was needed. Sure the apartment is only half an hour from the hospital."

"I know where it is." The words had slipped out before Adrienne thought it through. She did not want to hurt Patrick just now. In some ways she was pleased that he called her when he was in trouble, but she wanted to insist on where his priorities were at the moment: "You are with Sheila now, hard and all as it is or me to say it. She needs your support. You have to be there for her and the child."

"I'm not with Sheila," Patrick said.

"I know. They sent you home. I was listening."

"That's not what I mean. I am not with Sheila in that sense of the word. She is staying with her mother and father."

Adrienne wondered had she heard him correctly: "But you are taking responsibility for the child?"

"That is what had me at the hospital. We are not living together. We are not talking of getting married or anything."

"Why are you telling me this, Patrick?"

"I wanted you to know how things stand."

"I know how they stand," Adrienne assured him. "We are separated."

"That is not to say that we won't get back together."

Adrienne spoke slowly and as clearly as she could: "Listen to me, Patrick. You and I are separated and that is the beginning and the end of it. We will not be getting back together. I am not saying that to hurt you on this of all nights. I am glad you rang and that we can speak together as friends. But that is all there is to it."

"You have met someone else?"

"I hav met plenty, but that is all there was to it. We met on the street and walked on. I don't want to get close to any other man. In fact I want a break from every man in the world."

"Life is a bitch." Adrienne wondered had Patrick even listened to what she had been saying.

"You will have a different story tomorrow. You will be the father of a lovely little baby. Sheila will be alright and the sun will be shining again."

"Maybe," he conceded.

"Put back the lid on that bottle," Adrienne said, "and go to sleep. You will be no good to anyone in the condition you are in at the moment."

"I was just telling you how I feel," Patrick answered. "Isn't that what you wanted when we were together, that I would say what I feel."

Adrienne did not know how to reply to that: "It is to Sheila and the baby you will need to express your feelings from now on."

"That is what I am telling you. There is nothing between me and Sheila but the child, and that might not even be there in the morning."

Adrienne told him not to be talking like that: "Be positive, at least until you have reason not to be."

"It might be for the best."

"Have you drank the whole bottle?" Adrienne asked. "I have never heard you in such bad humour."

"People have always said that what is kept in when you are sober comes out when you are drunk."

"So you admit to being drunk?"

"I've had a few scoops," Patrick admitted.

"It is not the truth that comes out most of the time when a person is drunk," Adrienne said, "but paranoia. Don't be thinking of yourself so much but of your child and its mother."

"Haven't I been trying to tell you for the last hour . . ."

Adrienne interrupted him: I know what you have been telling me, because you have said it again and again. What I am saying to you that you need to accept responsibility for Sheila and the baby. Your baby. You have to accept it, even if it goes against the grain.

"I don't know why I called you at all," Patrick said. "I didn't realise you had become so hard, Adrienne. You usen't be like that."

"I'm not trying to be cruel, just telling it like it is. Go to bed now, Patrick. Say a prayer or something if you can that your baby will be alright."

Patrick hung up. Adrienne failed to sleep until well out into the night. The talk on the phone with her former husband swirled around in her head. She realised that the next day would be a write-off as far as work was concerned because of tiredness and worry. She had never heard Patrick so low before. She hoped he had gone to sleep. He sounded as if he was close to self harm. "That's the worst about being so far from home," was her final thought before she fell asleep.

xiii

GIORGIO'S SUSPICIONS WERE RAISED AS he approached his water-taxi in the morning. It looked as if there was some kind of graffiti scrawled on the tarpaulin that covered his boat. He walked towards it carefully, on full alert, to see what message had been left for him. His heart pounded as he realised how vulnerable he was as he walked into that open space without any kind of cover. He stood and looked around, his eyes combing every window in the buildings that were in the vicinity to see was he being watched, or worse still was he in the line of fire of a sniper. All of the windows just looked like mirrors as they reflected back the light of the morning sun.

Crouching down in the classic way to make him a smaller target for any rifle fire, Giorgio approached his boat. Suddenly he was laughing with relief when he saw that the white splash on the tarpaulin was bird droppings. That was not unusual as there were so many pigeons and seagulls in the area. "It's one thing to be scared shitless," he told himself, "bit it's worse to be scared by a bit of birdshit." He promised himself that he would not allow imaginary threats to get him so worked up. "If it is going to happen, it will just happen and it will all be over."

He had enjoyed the previous night in the Principe. He had a meal there and went to the bar afterwards for the music and singing. There was the inevitible group from one of the liners, Americans mostly, what were generally known as the blue rinse brigade. This group were from Pittsburg and had some great dancers of the waltz among them. They certainly knew how to enjoy themselves. One woman who was probably in her seventies dragged Giorgio out for a dance. Her friends kidded her about her toyboy. He was not a great dancer but she knew all the moves and led him around. They had some kind of common fund and he did not have to put a hand in his pocket to buy a drink all night.

He got talking to a man from the group who told him he had emigrated from Achill Island in the west of Ireland. His wife was from the next county, from a place called Maam. Giorgio never pretended to be anything other than Italian. The Irishman did not seem to think it was in any way strange that an Italian should ask him what part of the country of his birth had he come from. It was probably common enough in the United States to be asked such a question by ex-patriates, but hardly by people from another country.

At one stage of the night Giorgio felt that a burly middleaged man of the type you might see on secret service security for the President seemed to be watching him. Dressed in a tuxedo and wearing a dicky bow tie, he looked dapper and handsome. It was his fixed stare that worried Giorgio. He avoided those gimlet eyes as often as he could, but when he glanced back they seemed to be boring into him. He was relieved when he saw the man being led to the bathroom, and he realised that he was blind.

Looking at the stars on his way back to his apartment, Giorgio thought of the young Japanese woman to whom he had talked on the boat earlier that day. He wondered where she was. Having a meal by the banks of the Seine, he thought. She had reminded him of the girl from the same country who had once shared his bed and worn him out with the intensity of her lovemaking. He would give anything now, he thought, to have that same level of fatigue and for the same reason. "There is nothing between us except the Alps," he told himself ruefully.

Giorgio allowed Adrienne into his thoughts for the first time since he had left her outside her apartment complex. He had really messed up that evening. He was allowing paranoia to get the better of him. If he could only get another chance with her it would not matter if it was the top republican gunman or drug baron's hitman that was looking over his shoulder. He had only one life and why should he spend it worrying?

He decided he would make another effort to meet Adrienne. What had he to lose? The worst thing she could do was reject him, but at least he would have tried. He fell asleep with that thought in his mind and woke in the morning with the same thought. He had only one thing in his mind when he got up that morning, to try and meet Adrienne before the day was done. The streak of white droppings on the tarpaulin of his boat had shaken him for a while, but he was ready to get on with life again.

There was plenty of work ahead of Giorgio that morning. He had to bring the group from Pittsburg back to their cruiseliner, take another group from the airport, and bring an older couple with walking difficulties to the landing place closest to Saint Mark's Square. All of that would take half the day. The rest would depend on demand from hotels or whoever just turned up or waved him down while he was sailing empty.

As he drove by in his water-taxi Giorgio intended to cast a glance at people eating in the café's and trattoria along the waterside. He had noticed Adrienne in one of those previously and he wanted to give the impression that he has come across her accidentally. If that did not work he would just go to her apartment and ask her out. He had intended to forget about her but that was not proving to be easy. There was something very appealing about her and she was easy to talk to. Being from the same country and speaking a language with the same nuances was always a help.

The group from Pittsburg were in high good humour and it was obvious that they had been dealing with their hangovers in the most common manner in the world, better known as the hair of the dog. Not for the first time Giorgio marvelled at what a great life many older people with money had. Once again he thought of his mother and her limited life. He would have to find a way to see her before she died, that is if she was not dead already. "If she is not, the sight of me would probably kill her anyway," he thought. "She has probably spent the last few years mourning my death."

He remembered that Adrienne had said she hoped to go back to Ireland for an exhibition in Galway. The thought struck him that he might be able to go with her if they managed to get back together. There would be less suspicion of two people travelling together. He could use his Italian identity and speak in pidgin English. How, where and when he would get to see and meet his family would have to be worked out. The big problem was that it would be hard to prevent the secret of the dead man who was still alive from leaking out.

Such hopes and dreams had to be put on hold as he took his place in the queue beside the cruiseliner and gradually edged his way to the bottom of one of the many stairways lowered to cater for passengers exiting or entering the great liner. The woman who had danced with him came close to losing her life in a matter of seconds as she slipped while stepping from the water-taxi on to the stairway. In her panic she pushed the stair-rail from her which created a space between that and the boat. She plunged down into the black-green water and for a moment Giorgio was sure that she would be lost.

The biggest danger was that the water-taxi would swing in against the stairway and prevent her from surfacing. He put all his weight into keeping that space open and then he saw her grey head rising towards the surface. He grabbed hold of her hair and hauled her up. She had obviously been a swimmer and held her breath, because instead of being half-drowned by her ordeal she arrived on to the bottom of the stairway screaming and shouting and cursing at the cold water, something which caused more panic to her fellow passengers than to herself.

Stewards and security people soon arrived with blankets and what looked like a shroud of tinfoil to keep her warm at least until she would be able to change her clothes. Giorgio was never as satisfied to see the back of a cruiseliner as he was with that one. He wondered could she sue him, but she was probably happy enough to be alive and to leave it at that. "Why had they so much to drink before taking to the sea?" he wondered, as he headed on his next appointment towards the airport. "Nerves, maybe, or fear, or they just wanted to have a good time." The thought of his mother on such a cruise did not seem to appeal as much anymore. "She would be a lot happier going to Lourdes, he thought.

That suddenly seemed like a great idea. Why did he think he could only meet his family in Ireland? Who would expect to find a supposedly dead former sniper at a major shrine? The Virgin Mary might not approve, he thought, but then again maybe she would. She was not averse to the bit of fun. Only for her appeal to Jesus the crowd at the wedding of Cana would have had nothing to drink. Anyway wasn't it all supposed to be about forgiveness and reconciliation? He wondered how his family would feel if they found out that he was alive. The old question of whether they could keep a secret surfaced again in his mind.

They probably could, for the sake of seeing him again, and to save him from danger or death maybe. He wondered had they ever been hassled or threatened by drug barons whose hackles he had raised by his actions. He realised that he had a lot of thinking to do before coming to a decision on this matter. In the meantime he had a job to do, a living to earn. He had travelled the airport route so often that he could nearly find his way with his eyes closed. He always enjoyed the moment when on his own he could go to full throttle and let the horsepower send him leaping through and across the waves.

He could not do anything like that when he had passengers on board. Most of them were already scared as they were not used to boats. There was also the question of cost as more speed tended to mean more fuel being burnt. The other side to that was that getting a journey done quicker generally led to more passengers, more work, more money. He often wonered how a water-taxi would work ar home on Galway Bay, bringing people from the train station to Salthill for example, or across the Bay to Ballyvaughan. Who knows," he thought, but the day might come that I will be doing so, but I have a lot of hurdles to cross first."

For some time now Giorgio had been wondering how to get his case and the cases of others in the same position considered by the Ard-Chomhairle, the top echelon of the paramilitary organisation to which he belonged. He did not even know if they had survived the decomissioning of weapons and the supposed break-up of the movement. He really was in a Limbo if those who used to pull the strings no longer had any strings to pull.

Perhaps he should write to one of the alleged leaders now in elected politics north or south of the Irish border. Maybe it was better to stay 'dead.' Coming out of the closet was one thing, coming out of the coffin another.

Giorgio caught no sight of Adrienne as he travelled in and out of the canals that evening. When he finished work he want back to his apartment, took a shower, put on his best clothes and asked one of his mates to drop him outside her apartment block in his own water-taxi. He did not know which of the four apartments she lived in, but it should be easy enough to find out from the surnames next to the bells. The name with the 'Mac' was pretty obvious. He pressed the button. When she asked who was there, he told her who it was and she said: "Come on up."

"I'm sorry for the mess," she said when he entered the apartment. She had a paintbrush in one hand, a palette in the other. Her clothes were protected by a kind of smock-apron: "I was not expecting visitors."

"I didn't know whether to call or not," Giorgio said. "Everything seemed to fall apart on us the other night."

"Thanks for coming," she said. "I was not really expecting to see you again. Would you mind sitting down until I finish this? I won't be long. By the way would you like a glass of wine?"

"I wouldn't say no," he answered in the Irish manner.

"Do you mind getting it yourself? I'm covered in paint. There is a bottle of white in the fridge and two glasses on the sideboard."

xiv

GIORGIO SAT QUIETLY SIPPING HIS wine while Adrienne concentrated on her work. She said she would not be long, but if she did not finish the picture properly now, she might never do so. She would stand back from the canvas, which was turned away from him, from time to time. She would just seem to put a spot or a small ine on the painting before standing back again to observe, her head slightly to one side like a curious little bird.

"That's it," she said at last, putting her brushes into a jar with some liquid in it. She poured herself a glass of wine and sat opposite him, pulling her feet up under her on the small chair. "How are you?" she asked.

Giorgio answered her question with another one: "Can I look at the picture?"

Adrienne waved towards the canvas in a gesture of permission: "Feel free, so long as you tell me what you really think. I don't want some kind of false praise."

Giorgio stood looking at the painting for a while but could not make head or tail of it. He wondered what difference one spot or line of the kind he saw Adrienne add to it, made. It was all a mystery to him, an amalgam of lines and colours. He decided on a diplomatic answer: "The colours are nice."

Adrienne repeated the words: "The colours are nice," after him as though she was talking to a child.

"What do you want me to say?"

"I want your honest opinion, not some softsoap of an answer. Do you like the picture or do you not?"

Giorgio said: "I like it, but I haven't a clue what its supposed to be about."

"That's an honest answer, even if it is not necessarily what I would like to hear."

"Tell me what you want me to hear," he said with a smile, "and I will repeat it for you. To tell you the truth I know nothing about art." He told her about the conversation he had with the young woman from Japan and his assertion that she was interested only on the fact that it was by a famous artist, rather than in the quality of the picture itself.

"Interesting," Adrienne mused, a glint in her eye.

"What is interesting?"

"That you discuss art with young Japanese girls while out on the sea. Do you pay the same attention to the older women you ferry from one place to another?"

"Most of them don't have enough English," Giorgio said lightly, "and quite a few of them are deaf. In fact I speak to everyone who speaks to me. A taxi-driver has to be nice to all of his customers."

"You were not so nice to me the first time I met you, as one of your customers," Adrienne said, tongue in cheek.

"What did I do wrong?"

"You let me tumble on my back in an embarrassing position on the floor of the cabin."

"It was worth it for the view," Giorgio answered.

"I could have been injured and sued you for millions of euro."

"A person needs to hold on to something in a boat. I presumed that a young woman of the world knew that. I would know better now, particularly after what happened this morning." He told Adrienne of the woman who had fallen into the sea between his taxi and the liner. "She was old but she was gamey," he said. "You should have seen her dance. "I think she just fell in so that I would have to save her."

Adrienne nodded: "Mnnn . . ." Giorgio got the impression that she was not really listening to him. She got up and took the picture she had painted the previous day and left to dry in the bathroom and showed it to him: "What do you think of this one?"

"I like both of them," he said, "but I see very little difference between them."

"The difference between them is the difference between the sun rising and the sun setting."

Giorgio answered: "I don't see the sun in either of them."

"It is not so much the sun itself, but the sunshine and the effects, the result of sunshine."

"I have told you that I know nothing about art, and I know even less now after trying to understand those pictures. I'm just an oldfashioned bloke who likes a picture in which you can recognise something. The same as in a photograph."

"There is nothing wrong with that," Adrienne said, "and there are thousands of such pictures all over this city. Religious art mostly."

"I would like to learn about the absreact stuff," Giorgio said a little shamefacedly, "because I haven't got a clue. I would love if you could bring me to the Guggenheim and teach me what it is all about."

"I am not so sure about teaching you." Adrienne did not seem very sure of herself.

"Are you saying that I am thick?"

She tried to explain: "It's a way of looking at things."

"And you can't teach an old dog new tricks."

"We all get a little settled in our ways. You know the way children mix and match colours and care little about order or perspective in their pictures. It is hard to reverse the effects of what is basicaly classical education."

"All I am asking for is some little clue of what it is all about," Giorgio said. "I don't expect to become an art expert in my old age."

"I will come with you to the Guggenheim if you are really serious about it," Adrienne said. "What day are you free?"

They decided on the following Sunday, and sat more at ease with other discussing what each though of as safe subjects, not really revealing anything about themselves. They talked mainly of their own country and the state of that nation generally. Giorgio asked after a while whether Adrienne would like to go out with him for a meal.

"Do you not think that one disaster is enough for this week?"

"I deserve that answer," he said. "I was away over the top.

"Forget about it," Adrienne said. "I'm too tired to go out anywhere."

"I understand," Giorgio joked: "You have been wielding that paintbrush all day."

"I just did not sleep well last night."

"I'm sorry if I came between you and your sleep."

"Don't flatter yourself. It's just a bit of news I got from home about someone in danger of losing a baby."

"A friend of yours?" Giorgio asked.

"Not really a friend. Someone I know," Adrienne answered truthfully, but she had no notion of telling any of her business to a stranger. She stood up and got a menu she had taken with her from a local trattoria. "Why don't we just order something in?"

"Suits me," Giorgio answered.

He chose what he wanted and Adrienne made the order. Giorgio offered to go out to buy a bottle of wine. "I didn't bring one with me," he explained, "because I did not know what kind of a reception I would get, whether I would be shown the door or not."

Adrienne giggled like a little girl: "You can see the door anytime you want, but whether you will be let in or not is another matter."

"Maybe I should go for wine."

"Relax, I have a bottle here," Adrienne told him. "Next time maybe."

Giorgio sat down: "So there is going to be a next time?"

"I thought we had arranged to go to the Guggenheim on Sunday. One day at a time. Let's take it like that.

"That's fine with me."

"Two strangers far from home," Adrienne mused. "There is no reason why we can't get together for a chat from time to time."

Giorgio agreed, although he hoped for more than that: "Do you miss the old country?"

"I'm not long enough away really to miss anything except my friends.

I'll be going back for an exhibition brfore very long if I can keep painting the way I have been for the past few days."

"Will you be exhibiting on your own or sharing it with a group?" Giorgio asked.

"On my own." Adrienne explained that some works she had exhibited a year earlier in Wicklow had not sold so she would have them for this one as well as her new work.

"So the west will be getting the gluggers, the eggs that didn't hatch?" Giorgio regretted his comment when he saw the way that Adrienne looked at him. "I'm sorry, it's my idea of a joke."

"It was actually the better ones that didn't sell," she said, "because I was asking too much for them. I thought we were still in celtic tiger country. I hadn't learnt the lessons of the recession."

"Tell me if it's none of my business, but how much would you be looking for one of those that you showed me earlier?" Giorgio asked.

"You mean if I found someone stupid enough to buy them?"

"I didn't say so."

"A thousand, a thousand two hundred, maybe on a good night when a lot of wine had been drank. It depends on the buyer like anything else a person is trying to sell."

Giorgio gave a low whistle: "To earn that for one day's work" he said with wonder in his voice. "I am definitely in the wrong job."

"I didn't paint anything for most of last year," Adrienne said, quietly.

"Why?" Giorgio asked. "I would paint one every day of the year if I could get prices like that for them. You could make half a million euro every single year."

"You need inspiration."

"You had none until you came here?" he asked. "Or do you mean that you had none until you met me?"

Adrienne laughed: "That is what triggered it alright."

"How do I know that it's not me in the pictures but that I am not able to recognise myself in the abstract?" he joked.

"The invisible man," Adrienne said more seriously. "A good name for a spy or an underground policeman."

"That was a lie the last night," Giorgio said regretfully.

"It sounded like that, but you were definitely scared. You are on the run from someone or something?"

"It's a long story and a complicated one," Giorgio admitted, "and you would be better off not knowing."

"Try me," she said. "I have no intention of going out with a man that I know nothing about."

"I was just making it up about being a spy," Giorgio said, "making a big story about what was little more than a business disagreement."

Adrienne searched for the truth: "What kind of a disagreement? Was it with that man with the beard in the trattoria?"

"I had a disagreement with another water-taxi driver and it got out of hand. He jumped me in the queue, and I got mad with him because he thought he could do anything he liked because he was Italian."

Adrienne probed: "That man in the trattoria?"

"I thought he was one of the other bloke's heavies. Anyway it is all sorfed now. Can we talk about something else?"

"My mother always said that a liar needs to have a good memory."

"Do you not believe me?" Giorgio asked.

"Do you believe yourself?"

"I didn't tell you the truth because I didn't want to put you in danger."

"The truth is supposed to set you free," Adriene said."

"It doesn't set free someone who is supposed to be dead. That's what I really meant by being underground."

"What are you talking about?"

Giorgio told her the basic facts of his past, the sniping, the faked funeral, missing out on the amnesty, being a nonperson.

"Why should I believe that any more than the other stories?" Adrienne asked. "I thnk you are a wonderful example of Walter Mitty syndrome, someone who makes exorbitant claims about himself, and what is more, believes in them."

Giorgio opened his shirt and showed one of the slogans of the IRA, 'tiocfaidh ár lá' (Our day will come) written above a celtic cross. "It's ironic. Everybodies day came except my day. I was the fool left lost between two worlds."

Adrienne found it hard to conceal her distrust: "I don't know can I believe one word from your mouth."

"Do you want to hear the truth?"

"One more lie and you will never see me again."

"OK, I'll give you chapter and verse. I will give you the names of the people I shot. You can check the information on the Internet."

"I can't believe that I am here having a conversation with a killer."

"A soldier," Giorgio insisted.

"Self-styled," Adrienne said ruefully.

"The bottom line is that you don't believe me."

"There is a ring of truth about it, but why did you tell me so many lies in the beginning?"

"I was trying to protect you, to keep you out of danger."

"What danger? The war is supposed to be over."

"Have you heard one word I said?" Giorgio asked. Have you understood anything? There are people, dangerous people out there searching for me. People who want to kill me. If you are seen with me, you will be in danger too."

"They would have found you long ago if they were serious about it," Adrienne said dismissively.

"So far they have not had a clue where to look, but some day someone on holiday is likely to recognise me and spread the word."

Adrienne seemed anxious. She asked: "Do you really think that I am in danger too?"

"I sincerely hope that neither of us is in danger," Giorgio answered. "Looking on the bright side the war is over as you said. They might just let sleeping dogs, or should I say dead dogs lie."

"That's the way to look at it," Adrienne said. "Don't always fear the worst."

"A person has to be realistic too. I wish there was some way of finding out whether I am off the hook or not as far as the movement is concerned."

Adrienne asked what seemed like the obvious question: "Can you not just ring up and ask?"

"When I died, so-called, I was warned never to contact anyone in the business again under pain of death."

"So you think I was drawn into it as soon as you shared your secret?" Adrienne asked anxiously.

"That is why I didn't want to tell you the full story the last night. That is why I lied at first tonight. I didn't want to put you in danger."

What you are saying is that if that fellow that was behind you in the restaurant the other night was on the lookout for you, I was in the same danger as you were?"

Giorgio tried to explain: "He would not have done anything then, because he would be recognised. Assasination usually takes place in back alleys, or by a clean shot from an upstairs window. There would be little point in silencing just me if you know the whole story as well."

Adrienne looked him straight in the eye: "How many people have you killed because they were in the wrong place in the wrong time?"

"Nobody," he answered confidantly. "My work was done from a distance, and I was good at my job. I hit the target every time. I can honestly say that there was never any collateral damage."

"The target," Adrienne said sarcastically. "What you hit was a non-person so? Just a target.

Giorgio answered calmly: "Exactly. I'm not proud of it. It was a war. A war for Ireland's cause, and for all the people who were trampled underfoot down through the centuries."

"The amazing thing is that you actually believe that," Adrienne said. "What about the Irish people whose allegience is to Britain? Have they no rights in all of this?"

"Look at the way they treated our people before and during the Civil Rights campaign. Gerrymandering, giving the new houses and jobs to their own. Our people were secondclass citizens."

"That justifies all the killing and the bombing?" Adrienne asked.

"There is nobody as happy as I am that they managed some kind of a settlement," Giorgio answered, "Except so far as they forgot about me. The question is would we have any kind of settlement except for what went on before? It was those spectaculars in London, Canary Wharf and those bombings that brought them to the table."

Adrienne sat uncomfortably without saying anything for some time. She eventually broke her silence with the words: "I never thought I would be sitting in the same room with a man who admitted to killing others."

Giorgio shrugged: "What happened happened."

There was a call on the intercom. Their takeaway dinners were being delivered. Adrienne and Giorgio ate in virtual silence, apart from praising the food, "I have a question for you," Adrienne said when they were nearly finished eating: "Would you do it again?"

Giorgio collected his thoughts before answering: "If I was the same age and in the same circumstances, I probably would. Right now I feel that it might have all been sorted politically without half the trouble. It's back to the old question: Was the 1916 Rising justified when Home Rule was on the way anyway?"

"What do you think?" Adrienne asked.

"They just ended up with the same thing and a civil war as well."

"So it was all for nothing in both cases?"

"I didn't say that," Giorgio replied. "It happened because people felt driven to it, because they were impatient and saw no other way."

Adrienne held Giorgio's gaze: "Would you kill again?"

"If my life and the life of someone I loved was in danger, I would have no other choice," he answered.

"Who do you love?"

"Myself of course," he replied. "That goes without saying."

"Don't be facetious."

Giorgio did not answer for a few moments. The easy thing to say would be 'You,' but that would not be appropriate after what he had revealed about himself. "I haven't seen my mother or the rest of my family for a long time. They don't even know that I am alive. You don't stop caring for your own."

"You are hard work," Adrienne said with a shake of her head.

"How do you mean?"

"I mean that I like you. I can't say that I know you, but I feel drawn to you. After what I have heard, I don't know."

"I like you too. That should be obvious."

"Don't say that you like me just because I said it to you."

"I wouldn't be here if I didn't," Giorgio said.

"So what do we do now?"

"Would you come with me to the Guggenheim on Sunday, like we said earlier?" Giorgio asked. "We could see how we feel then."

"It probably wouldn't do any harm."

"If you want to leave it, that's ok too," Giorgio said quietly. "I know what I told you earlier scared you a little."

"It scared me a lot."

"Still if old enemies can sit down together to run the country in Stormont Castle in Belfast . . ."

Adrienne did not give him time to finish: "It's the killings, the murder I am finding it hard to deal with. I'll need to think hard about it between now and Sunday."

"For what it's worth I regret ever having to kill anyone. Especially for the wives and children left without a father, but there is nothing I can do now to bring them back to their famlies."

"What made you start in the first place?" Adrienne asked.

"Idealism. Misplaced idealism maybe. I understand why young men and women go out with bombs tied around them in the Middle East and further afield. Because they are young, idealstic and probably brainwashed. And there are older armchair generals cynical enough to send them out to their deaths for the sake of the cause."

Adrienne wondered out loud: "For all we know those generals are not cynical at all, but idealistic and passionate themselves."

"They should be the ones risking their lives so."

"I admire idealsm even though I was never blessed with much of it myself," Adrienne said. "What I actually like most about you is that you are not like many of your, of our generation."

"I'm a generation older than you," Giorgio asured her. "Keep talking. What is it that you like about me?"

"You don't seem to be interested in making money, in amassing a fortune, in owning a stack of houses and apartments, all of the things that drove our own little country into the ground."

"I try to earn the odd euro, the same as the next man." Giorgio said.

"Your whole life is not concentrated on making money. It never was or you would not be where you are now."

"You must be an angel from heaven yourself," Giorgio suggested when they had finished the bottle of wine and opened another. "I have bared all, told you all my faults and failings. The only thing that I know so far about you is that you are an artist."

"I have not killed anybody," she answered. When she saw Giorgio wince, she decided to lighten things a little. "I have not killed anyone yet. But be careful." She was silent for a moment. "I am not trying to diminish what you have told me, because it has certainly shaken me." She went on to tell him about her life, her mother's death, about her marriage to Patrick, Sheila carrying his child, her separation and hoped for divorce. "the typical lfe of a woman," she said, "in the early stages of this century, this millennium."

"I can understand why you mght want to kill someone," Giorgio said, after hearing about Patrick and Sheila.

"As far as Patrick is concerned," Adrienne told him, "divorce is worse than murder, so I am not sure what is going to happen in that regard."

"He has hurt you a lot?"

"I completely lost confidence," Adrienne admitted. "I have done no work for a long time before coming here."

"I hope what I have told you has not affected you too much," Giorgio commented. "You needed to hear the truth."

"I don't think that anything I hear will affect me too much anymore, because I will not allow anyone to hurt me to that extent ever again."

Adrienne's phone rang, but she told Giorgio that she did not want to answer it. When it rang again and again she picked it up. It was Sheila and she seemed to be upset. Adrienne tried her best to be civil: "Sheila! This is a big surprise."

Giorgio stood up, ready to leave the room and let her have her privacy but Adrienne signalled him to sit down.

Sheila dispensed with the pleasanteries: "Do you know where Patrick is?" she asked.

"How would I know?" Adrienne remembered her worries after speaking to him. A cold sweat seemed to be breaking out on the back of her neck and across her shoulders.

"He didn't come in to the hospital at all this evening."

"I presume you have tried his mobile."

"Do you think that I'm stupid?"

Adrienne suppressed her urge to say "I do." Instead she answered: "He rang me just after you were admitted. He was worried about you and the baby. He sounded stressed really."

"He is obviously not stressed enough to check how we are," Sheila replied angrily.

"How is the baby by the way?" Adrienne asked gingerly.

"Alright, it seems. They are keeping us monitored. That is all that they are saying. Everything was going fine until Patrick disappeared."

"Did he go to work today?" Adrienne remembered how depressed he had sounded.

"I was talking to him in the office and he said he would come in here when he finished work."

"Maybe he went for a bite to eat, or for a drink."

Sheila almost shouted: "For four hours?"

"He had a lot drank last night," Adrienne answered, "and he sounded very depressed. As low as I have ever heard him. I don't think he would have even called me if he was not feeling so badly."

Sheila clearly resented the fact that he would have rung his ex-wife: "For all I know he could be calling you all the time, because he never stops talking about you."

"I have moved on," Adrienne told her. "That part of my life is over and we won't be getting back together. That is not to say that I am not worried when he sounds like he sounded last night."

"A pity Patrick doesn't know that you think it's over."

"It's not that I have not told him often enough. I told him last night to concentrate all his energies from now on on you and the baby."

The call ended abruptly: "Here he is now," Sheila said and switched off her phone.

Adrienne stood looking at her mobile: "And goodbye to you too. No yes, no or thank you. I don't know what he sees in her."

"A free ride last year," Giorgio said lightly. "A pain in the arse this year, the story of the human race."

"Aren't you the philosopher," Adrienne commented. "Is that how you look at all women? Trouble, once you have had your oats?"

"That is not how I look at you. Just beauty and intellgence, today, tomorrow and the next day."

"If you only meant a word of it."

"I heard every word," Giorgio said, "because you were on loudspeaker. I gather your man has been found safe and well."

Adrienne sounded as if she was talkng to herself: "Is anyone ever able to leave the past behind them?"

"Isn't that what we were talking about all evaning? We all carry the lives we have led the way a snail carries its house on its back. Anyway I'll see you on Sunday, if that is still on." He stood up and put on his tunic.

Adrienne held up the bottle: "One for the road, or should I say one for the river?"

"You won't get any work done tomorrow," Giorgio said, holding out his glass for a refill.

"I will just be messing about with paint, but you will have to drive your speedboat to and from the airport."

"I will be alright after a night's sleep," he said.

"Is there any danger of getting breathalysed?" Adrienne asked.

Giorgio explained that he had not brought his water-taxi: "I will call one of my mates to pick me up. I didn't want to leave my boat tied up outside all night."

"Thank you for proctecting my reputation," Adrienne joked. "It would be better, of course, to have a gondola parked outside. Those fine strapping men with striped shirts would appeal to any woman."

"I will have to buy such a shirt," Giorgio said. "They sell them in most of the shops along with the masks."

"It's not the shirt that makes the man, however."

Speaking of men," Giorgio said. "Yourself and Patrick, your husband still seem cosy enough form what I have heard there."

"Do you think you need to take him out?"

"Not while he has that one that was on the phone to control him."

Adrienne corrected his earlier statement: "Patrick is not my husband. He is my ex. You can't just throw ten years of marriage on the dungheap. We are part of each other's history. I have to admit I was worried when I heard that he was mssing. Of course he was not missing at all except in the head of that little butterfly that is carrying his baby. She probably thought that he had come out here to see me. It would have been good enough for her."

"You are still angry because of it all?"

"Why wouldn't I? Adrienne asked. "If the bitch could even be civil. She can't even say: "Hello or goodbye," just "where is he?"

"Do you think they will marry?

"I don't know and I don't care. It's none of my business anymore. I am not going back to Patrick, whatever he thinks. I don't think that he should marry her, but he is that kind of a sentimental fool that is likely to marry her out of duty, because of the child."

Giorgio enquired: "Has he asked you to go back to him?"

"He did last night, when he was drunk and lonely and worried about his child. I made it clear that I have started my new life without him and that there will be no going back."

Giorgio mangled his Shakespeare: "Methinks that she protests too much and too often."

"She protests too much because nobody seems prepared to believe her when she says that she is not going back."

"Everybody has their own baggage."

Adrienne suddenly started to laugh: "I don't think Patrick would be too pleased to be described as baggage. But you are right. We are all like those snails you talk about. Seilimidges we used to call them, carrying our worlds, real and imaginary on our backs."

When Giorgio finished his glass of wine, Adrienne made no effort to detain him. She was tempted to ask him to stay, but she felt that it was too soon, especially after what he had told her earlier. He made half an effort to kiss her, but she offered her cheek rather than her lips.

XV

GIORGIO DECIDED NOT TO CALL anyone to collect him from Adrienne's apartment. He followed the narrow lanes and footpaths. He did not feel that he was in any way drunk even though he had consumed more than a bottle of wine. There were few people on the streets or lanes at that time. Most seemed to be in a hurry, probably returning home from late night jobs in the tourist industry. Boats still chugged up and down the canal, mostly of the vaperetto variety, though some water-taxis still sped through the traffic. Cairbineri boats had their sirens going like police-cars in other cities. They seemed to be busy on the night, but that probably contributed to the safety of walkers like himself. He felt no fear in that regard, as casual theives would likely be no match for a man with paramilitary training.

Events of the evening went through Giorgio's mind instead of the sleep he hoped for when he lay on his bed. He was pleased hat he had told the truth, or much of it anyway, to Adrienne. He was afraid however that both of them mght be in danger because of it. Would she be able to keep her mouth shut about this Irishman she had met far from home? What about when she was gossiping with her friends when she went back for that exhibition? There would be the inevitible questions about her lovelife and whom had she met in the city of romance.

If all went well the two of them might be a couple, might be partners by then. The other women would be quizzing her about what kind of a man he was. He wondered should he take a chance and go back to Ireland with her, to test the waters on where he really stood. Where he stood with her and where he stood in so far as the movement was concerned. He wouldn't be going back to meet his family this time, even though he would love to do so, not to speak of seeing his home and his part of the country again. He would soon find out what if any danger he was in, or was all his worrying on that score for nothing.

Giorgio had drifted into sleep when he awoke with a start. He was sure that he had heard soft footsteps and that they had stopped outside the door of his apartment. There were low whispers. It was as if there were two or more people outside his door, preparing to break in. He reached for the revolver that lay under his pillow every night, removed the safety clip and moved slowly towards the door. He stood to one side in order to see his possible assailants before they saw him. He was on full alert as he tried to listen to the whispered conversations outside.

At this stage there did not seem to be a risk of an imminent attack. Giorgio placed his gun within easy reach on the bed and slipped into his t-shirt and trousers. He approached the door again, the gun in his right hand, pointing towards the ceiling. He opened the door stealthily but quickly hid the gun when he realised who was there. It was the postman. His back was turned to Giorgio and he was talking quietly on his mobile phone. He turned around when he heard the apartment door open. Giorgio asked was their mail for him and when the postman said no, he quickly closed the door. He checked his watch and it was seven in the morning. He had slept for far longer than he realised. The postman was not early. He was late. It was time to get up and get ready for work.

Giorgio was pleased that the other man had not seen his gun. He would most likely have told the police about this cowboy that was staying in one of the apartments. That would just attract attention and questions. "What kind of a fool am I?" he asked himself. He put on his shoes so that he would be available if anyone called for a taxi. He then stretched on top of his bed to catch up on lost sleep as well as to get rid of his hangover. It was almost twelve o'clock when they rang from Hotel Principe asking him to collect a group from the Lido.

Giorgio was soon wide awake and driving his boat against the blustery wind which was blowing drops of rain. The open sea journry to and from the Lido was easy compared to winding left and right in the main canal to avoid vaperettos and gondolas. His cargo were a group of Oxford Dons in so far as he could make out. They were quiet and reserved, more like the Japanese than the Americans whom he had taken from place to place in the recent past.

Giorgio was somewhat relieved to find that none of this group seemed interested in chatting to their water-taxi driver. It occurred to him that one of their sons could be one of the British soldiers he had taken out with a sniper's bullet. The young man's parents could be there in his boat, completely ignorant of the fact that their driver had killed their son. He had nothing against the British as long as they stayed out of the affairs of his home country. He recalled something he had read in Ernie O'Malley's book "*On Another Man's Wound*," about the author enjoying Shakespearian sonnets one evening, while citizens of the gteat bard's country were being killed hy him the following day.

As far as Giorgio was concerned, this was a way of saying: "Nothing personal, but you are in the wrong country. Clear out and we will be satisfied. We enjoy your literature and your drama, your television soapoperas, your soccer teams, your pop groups, your great orchestras, your comedians, but we like to have our own political freedom." That was how he had felt during his sniper days. He had a job to do, a war to win, and God help anyone who came in his way, accidentally or otherwise, while trying to do so.

The facts of the present case of course were that Giorgio's passengers probably had no connection at all with the British Army, and if they had it would be with the officer classes, not the ordinary workingclass private who had 'joined the army to see the world,' as the advertisements used to say. The only world most of them got to see in their stint in Northern Ireland was a divided and bitter one, people separated on seemingly religious lines in an increasingly secular world. The arrived, ostensibly to bring peace, but found themselves the enemy, enmity exascerbated by army atrocities like the Bloody Sunday massacre in Derry.

"Enough of the past," Giorgio told himself as his boat hopped off the backwash of the vaperetto in front of him. "Concentrate on the future." He was looking forward to going to the Guggenheim with Adrienne. He looked across at that gallery as they sped past. There were people on the steps admiring the sculptures outside. Whatever was to happen between himself and Adrienne, Giorgio thought, it would be no weight for his mind to learn a bit more about art, and especially about the type of picture that he could see no sense or reason in.

He thought again of writer and revolutionary, Ernie O'Malley, learning about art after years as a Republican soldier. It proved that there was life after the war, whatever about life after death. He himself would love to learn to paint and to carve, he thought, if he got that opportunity. It would certainly be worthwhile to learn more about the subject. What was the point in being in the city of art and not knowing anything about it?

Giorgio had more time to think when his Oxford tourists were ashore, seeing the sights and having a meal. As he stretched in the sun on top of the cabin of his speedboat, he was no longer Giorgio. He was Paul and he was at the bottom of the clff known as Aill na bPeist. He and his brother Morgan were picking winkles and gathering mussels.

94

They came across bones which they presumed belonged to some animal that was washed ashore or had fallen from the cliff. They used the ribs as swords as they fought pretend battles as pirates and seamen. When they went back later to collect more of the bones for the same purpose, they had been washed away by the tide. That did not bother them too much as they were able to now use sea rods as swords and rifles.

Searods were soft, but bones were hard. They still had the first two bones they had taken from the body. They were relatively short and curved, reminding him of scimitars seen in comics as Arab raiders swarmed into a ship. He was struck on the side of the head with one of them and looking back now he was probably concussed. He had passed out and Morgan had been distraught. They said at home that he had fallen and hit his head on a stone, which explained the swelling. It had never occurred to him that those could have been human bones until he had strange dreams afterwards. It was as if his feet were caught in a fishing net. He was underwater trying to escape from it, but he was unable to escape. He woke up in a sweat just as his breath as running out.

This convinced Giorgio that the bones were human and belonged to a drowned fisherman. He knew such bones should have a Christian burial, but by now they were scattered all over the place or washed out to sea. Morgan and himself had gone back but found only a piece of torn clothing. Years later he had heard Morgan telling that story in a pub as if it was he who was the victim who had been hit on the head, as if the drowning dream was his and not his brother's. He had lost his cool and struch Morgan in the jaw because he had stolen his story. They had laughed about it later because it had all seemed so stupid.

What had surprised him most was that Morgan had actually thought that he was the one hurt, that he was the dreamer. They had talked about it so much between themselves and kept it their secret that it had come to belong equqlly to both of them. As he lay in the sun on the cabin of his boat Giorgio wondered why should such thoughts come to him now in a city far from home. Perhaps it was the smell of the sea. There was something about it which always reminded him of where he had come from.

Giorgio had often wondered why the soldiers and drug barons he had killed never returned to haunt his dreams or to give him nghtmares. He was glad that they didn't. As a child he had lit candles in the local church for the drowned sailor. What if they had got it all wrong? They had found no skull. The bones might have been of a sheep or an old donkey that had fallen over the cliff. It may have been something else completely, most likely the blow on his head which had led to such dreams.

Giorgio was still thinking of bones as he drove his boat past the *Simitario*, the island in which most citizens of Venice are buried. San Michele is the correct name of the place, but Simitario is the name of the vaperetto stop, the little pier at the gates or doors of the cemetery. It amazed him the first day he had gone ashore there. The place was full of graves and ossuarys in which the bones of the dead were kept. These bones were removed from graves to make room for other burials and kept in what looked like huge chests of drawers. In fairness to the people of the place or the workers who were responsible, the cemetery island was beautifully maintained, with flowers of every kind growing all over the place.

The return of his group of tourists awoke Giorgio from his daydreams. It was as if their wanderings through the historic buildings and their meal afterwards had given them a new lease of life. They were talkative and friendly, gently ribbing one of their members whose cardigan had been bombed with the droppings of a passing dove. "*Where there's muck, there's luck,*" Giorgio said in a mock attempt to sound like an Italan speaking English. Most of them had never heard that figure of speech, so he advised the woman in question to: "Buy lotto."

xvi

As soon as Giorgio left her apartment the previous night, Adrienne rang her former husband, Patrick. She had not wanted to do so while Giorgio was present. She was still unsure of this new man who had come into her life. Was he telling the truth? Was he just showing off in a Walter Mitty fashion, creating a life for himself that would make him seem important? Still his final story had a ring of truth from what she had been aware of down through the years of the movement to which he had belonged. She felt she still had a lot of thinking to do before really letting him into her life.

She was well aware that it was late, but after talking earlier to Sheila she was worried about Patrick's state of mind. He was not very pleased when he was awakened by the phone, saying he would have ignored it except that it might have something to do with the baby whose life still seemed to be in danger.

"I am sorry to be ringing so late," Adrienne apologised, "but I was worried about you since Sheila rang."

This came as a surprise to Patrick: "You mean to say that Sheila rang you? What did she do that for?"

"She thought I mght know where you were, since you had not gone to the hospital as arranged."

"I did go to the hospital."

"That was much later than you said you would," Adrienne told him. "About four hours later. She was sick with worry or she would not have rung me. You just arrived as she was talking to me."

"You know more about what is happening in this country than I do," Patrick answered.

"What happened? What delayed you for that long?"

"Is it any of your business?" he asked. "You are the one who is always telling me that my life has nothing to do with you."

"I was worried after the state you were in the night before."

"This evening was all a misunderstanding," Patrick said. "Sheila thought I had said one thing, and I thought another."

97

"Not much communication there." Adrienne regretted saying so as soon as the words were out of her mouth.

"Not much communication here either," Patrick commented. "You didn't listen much when we were together, and you don't seem to have learned much since."

"That is a very cruel thing to say."

"The truth is bitter, as the old language used to put it."

"Anyhow this is not about me but about you," Adrienne asserted herself. "You could have phoned her."

"I had important meetings. I sent her a text but her phone was powered off to let her sleep. I was worried myself when she did not text back."

Adrienne could not resist a dig at the woman who in her eyes had stolen her husband: "I presume she is literate."

"Sheila is very intelligent."

"Looks can be decieving, I suppose," Adrienne commented.

"You think she looks stupid?"

"The jury is out on that one."

Patrick tried to be diplomatic: "This is not a competition between the two of you."

"If it is," Adrienne said ruefully, "she has won the jackpot."

"Some jackpot."

"You were not the worst, I suppose."

"Why did you leave it so late to ring?" Patrick asked.

"I thought that you would be at the hospital until now,"

"They threw me out a long time ago because they felt that Sheila needed to sleep."

"She could do with a bit of beauty sleep alright," Adrienne said lightly.

"Bitching doesn't suit you. You are not lonesome by any chance?"

"The truth is that I had dinner with a person who did not leave until half an hour ago," Adrienne said. "That is why I am so late calling you."

"Male company or female?"

"None of your business."

"Whatever makes you happy," Patrick said easily.

"Don't let it bother you,"

"It won't. I presume it was a gentleman?"

"Just a little pastime," Adrienne said, "A nice meal. A bottle of wine. You know yourself?"

And he is gone home already or you wouldn't be calling me. Now that is a gentleman."

Adrienne felt as if she was flirting with her former husband at this stage: "He came early and he was worn out and needed a night's sleep. You know how it is?"

"I think that you are making it all up as a cover for your loneliness," Patrick suggested.

"Believe what you like. I have not even the slightest touch of loneliness. This is the best move I have ever made. I have not been as happy for a long time. I am back working. I have painted a couple of pictures in the last few days. I have a new man in my life. I could not be happier."

"You rang me to tell me all that?" Patrick asked.

"As I said earlier, I rang because I was worried about you."

"Because you felt guilty?"

"What have I to feel guilty about?"

"According to yourself you are on the cusp of committing adultery if you have not done so already. Basically, I think you rang me looking for some kind of forgiveness or approval. Looking for my blessing."

"You didn't look for my blessing when you went at it hammer and tongs with that little mouse. Like two bunny rabbits."

Patrick laughed: "You have a fertile imagination."

"It wasn't your imagination that was fertile." Adrienne told him"

"Tell me about this new man."

"He is a few years older than me. About forty. Tall and fit. Greying slightly at the temples. A pleasant personality."

"A typical Italian gigilo, you mean."

"Did I say that he was Italan?"

"Where is he from so?" Patrick asked.

"He is a man of the world."

"Was it in this life you found this saint out of heaven, or had you to go to Nirvana for him?" Patrick wondered.

"You didn't think that I could get any man."

"You are a one man woman," her former husband observed. "I knew that from the first day I set eyes on you."

"And you think that you are that one man?" Adrienne said with some sarcasm.

"I would put a bet on it that you have not been with any other man but me in your life," Patrick asserted confidantly. "It would take a lot for you to change that, despite the way I let you down with Sheila. You are an oldfashioned girl at the back of it all."

"You think you know me well, but wait until you see." Adrienne was surprised at how well he actually seemed to know her, but she was not going to let him know that."

"The battle is not yet lost," he said. "You will come back to me when you get tired of that place."

Adrienne was getting annoyed: "Believe what you want to believe. Keep living in the world of make believe if you want to."

Patrick seemed to be growing in confidence: "You wouldn't be ringing me in the middle of the night, and I wouldn't be lying awake talking to you unless there is a chance of us getting back together again."

Adrienne did not put a tooth on it this time: "I rang because I thought you were contemplating suicide the last time we talked. I nearly gave your number to the Samaritans to ring you up and talk you out of it."

"Me!" Patrick almost shouted as if it was the last thing he could think of: "Don't give my number to anyone without my permission."

"You sounded as if you were in a black pit of depression."

"I had a little too much to drink. That was all."

"I'm glad that you got over it, but you had me scared. It sounded as if Sheila and the baby were just millstones around your neck."

"You were not far off the mark," Patrick replied, "but that was then and this is now. Getting her up the pole was a mistake, a mistake I will regret for the rest of my life. How often do I have to say I'm sorry?"

"Adrienne warned: "Don't let that child ever hear itself being called a mistake."

"I'm not that stupid, but when it was in danger of death the other day I thought that there is a God, that the right thing was about to happen. At the same time when I really thought about it, I realised that I didn't really want her to lose it."

"Maybe that is your god," Adrienne said quietly. "That child could be the making of you, the little god you helped to create, even if it was for the wrong reason."

"I would give anything for it to be ours," Patrick said, longingly, "and maybe it is not too late for that to happen yet."

"You didn't want children at the beginning," Adrienne reminded him."

"We were as poor as church mice at the time. What chance would a child have coming into the world in circumstances like that?

"Thousands did, and they managed. It is a long time since we were poor. We had plenty of money during the celtic tiger days, but there was no talk of having children then."

"You stayed on the pill." Patrick said.

"That was because you always wanted to wait another while. It didn't take you long to put that one up the spout when it suited you." There was poison in Adrienne's voice.

Patrick was getting uncomfortable and impatient: "We have had this conversation a hundred times before. Do we need to have it now in the middle of the night when a man has to get up and go to work early in the morning?"

"I will be getting up too."

"In your own time. You can decide to have a lie-in if you want."

Adrienne was not letting him away with anything: "You never believed that women did any work."

"I'm not saying that you don't work hard from time to time, but that you can start painting any time that suits you."

"It was a good day for both of us that we separated," Adrienne said, "because we could never agree about anything."

"Love lives on, despite argumants."

"Until unfaithfulness puts an end to it." Adrienne switched off her phone and dropped it as if it was a hot brick. She was sorry she had ever rang Patrick. She was trying to be kind and ended up angry and frustrated. She knew that she was not going to sleep much that night either. Her mind felt as if there was a whirlwind inside it. What really annoyed her was that Patrick would probably lie back on his pillow, forget about it all and fall asleep, pleased with himself that he had thrown a few spanners into her works.

Adrienne stood out on her balcony and looked down on a city that was not sleeping any more than herself. The boats chugged hither and thither. There were people on the streets and in the lanes, dogs barking, even birds singing here and there in the sparse foliage of the place. "Why can I not find a sensible, easygoing, innocent man without any kind of baggage?" she thought.

A spark of humour entered her mind and eased the gloom. She tried to imagine the type of man that would please her: "fit, wellbuilt, dumb, and great in bed. That would do me." For the first time since leaving Patrick she felt that she missed the physical side of love and the pleasure and satisfaction that provided. "What about an Italian stallion? She asked herself. Laughing quietly she thought: "I could do with one right now. A stallion that I could return to the stable when the job was done."

It was at times like this that Adrienne missed cigarettes most. As she looked out over the city, with a gentle and warm breeze tugging lightly at her hair, she thought she would love to have a cigarette in her hand, to be drawing the smoke gently down to her lungs and expelling it slowly. That would give her satisfaction, but she had nothing to smoke. She drew the air slowly in through her mouth as if drawing in tobacco smoke and exhaled slowly again and again. She felt better so she put Giorgio and Patrick and everything that bothered her out of her mind. She thought of the next picture she intended to paint, a picture that would attempt to capture the atmosphere of Venice from a balcony in the middle of the night. That gave her a possible title for a future exhibition: "Views from a balcony." She knew then that she was ready to sleep.

xvii

Giorgio had butterflies in his stomach on Sunday morning as he prepared to go to the Guggenheim gallery with Adrienne. As he dressed in his best clothes he was reminded of getting ready for mass when he was a boy. His mother would always insist that his shoes were polished and his clothes clean at least until they reached the church. There was even more readying to do when he was a mass-server. His little attache-case with surplice and soutane was readied the previous day.

His mother had a saying that part of every Saturday was fine, "to dry the priest's shirt." In fact he never remembered a Saturday which was wet from morning till night, and he had often hoped to prove the old statement wrong. What amazed him most as a child was that the priest could not afford a second shirt, given that a basket was passed around each Sunday to collect money. It was no wonder that there was often a stale smell from the priest's black clothes, a smell that seemed to be a mixture of cigarette smoke and church incense. At the time he had presumed that this was a holy smell.

"It is a long way between then and now," Giorgio thought. He had not darkened a church door for years, except to look at paintings now and again since coming to Venice. The last mass he was involved in was his supposedly funeral mass, where bags of sand provided ballast in the coffin in which he was supposed to be. When he was young he could not have imagined life without God or religion. He did not miss anything about it, except occasionally the music maybe or the smell of incense.

Giorgio had often thought that something died inside him the day he killed his first soldier. He had expected some kind of satisfaction, not from the killing but from hitting his first real target, finishing his task. In fact all he had felt was a kind of disgust with himself. The volunteer leader at the time had told him that feelings that had to do with conscience would dissipate after a while, that the soldier he shot would be no more to him than shooting a rabbit or a fox that was worrying sheep or stealing lambs. How right he was.

His heart had hardened little by little. He has used the atrocities committed by the other side to satisfy his conscience with regard to his sniping. As soon as he heard of a beating given by soldiers or police at a checkpoint or in a station, he was ready for his next target. He wanted to make them suffer. He would not listen to the radio or watch television for a week after a hit in case the reaction would upset him. He hated condemnations from church or political leaders as well as so-called 'right minded people.' Could they not understand that an Irish sniper was as much a soldier as a member of the British Army? The church in which he had grown up was prepared to bless soldiers going off to war in Vietnam, the Falklands or later in Iraq or Afghanistan, but there was no talk of blessing guerilla volunteers who were taking on an Empire on behalf of their own people. Was it any wonder that he lost all trust and faith in religion?

That is the way it always was and always will be, Giorgio thought. The volunteers who were involved in the Easter Rising of 1916 had been condemned too, but the day came when they were not just praised but adulated. There was a plaque in his local church which thanked the Old IRA for paying for the altar rails, while the same people had been threatened with or had been excommunicated by the same church years earlier. They had refused to allow the national flag, the tricolour, to be placed on his own coffin in the same church. It was only a mock funeral but the priest or people did not know that.

Giorgio shook himself out of his daydream. All of this mind wandering had come from readying himself on a Sunday morning, not for a communion service but for a date with a woman. He reminded himself that his mind should be on the present and the future, not on the past. A beautiful young vibrant woman was ready to spend the day with him, and here he was thinking of past hurts and battles lost and won. "Let go of the past and welcome the world," he told himself.

Adrienne looked lovely, Giorgio thought, in a light blue dress. She wore low shoes, the lessons of the cobbled streets well learned. It seemed as if she almost floated over the ground. It was a beautiful sunny day, the type of weather that raised most hearts. He reached for Adrienne's hand so that they would not get separated in the crowds that filled the streets. He was pleased with the way her hand held on tightly to his, in a gesture of friendship he felt, more than merely holding on. He had not brought his boat, to get a break from the driving drudgery of every day.

They took a vaperetto beneath the great bridges until they reached the small landing place closest to the Guggenheim gallery. There seemed to be more people everywhere on the Sunday than any other day. It was not just tourists in so far as they could make out, but local people as well, which seemed to give the city a more natural atmosphere. There was a long queue at the entrance to the gallery. The attendants were slowed down by the fact that they had to take people's handbags and store them while they were in the building. Safety precautions in case of bombings, according to the posters. Having been there earlier in the week, Adrienne had enough sense not to bring her handbag with her on that day.

"What will you do if you need to put on your face again?" Giorgio joked. "A woman without her handbag must be like a man without something else I dare not mention."

Adrienne said.: "I rarely wear paint or plaster of that kind, in case you hadn't noticed. Far from botox I was reared."

"Needless to say you don't need it."

"The crow's feet are there," she said, "but ageing is a natural part of everyone's life."

"Not mine," Giorgio joked. "I still look like a young lad."

"A bit of a lad alright," Adrienne commented. "One of those lads who like their lager and take women for granted."

"I'm not like that. I love women."

"Yeah," Adrienne said: "Love them and leave them."

"Don't judge me if you don't know me. Did I make any move the last night when I was in your place? It never crossed my mind."

Adrienne laughed: "If it didn't, there must be something wrong with you."

"So that is what you were thinking?" he said. "There was I, as innocent as anything, and you were gagging for it. Why didn't you make a move?"

"A woman, especially a lady, has more class than that. We only think of what is noble and beautiful."

"There is nothing much nicer than what I was referring to," Giorgio said, "if I remembe correctly."

"I doubt if you are very long deprived of female company at any stage," was Adrienne's reply.

"At the present time I am only interested in one woman."

"One woman at a time, I suppose, one today and another one tomorrow."

The queue moved on slowly. Some people grew frustrated with the wait and just went away, which allowed Adrienne and Giorgio to advance a few steps further.

"This is probably a bit of a chore for you," Giorgio said. "You are probably tired coming here. Have you visited all the museums and galleries in the city by now?"

"Quite a few, there are many still out there waiting for me, churches especially, some of which have extremely old paintings, but they are not always open when I get to them. There are also little galleries on street corners wher you can see new work."

"Abstract stuff, I suppose," Giorgio said. "Like your own."

"There is absolutely no art like mine anywhere in the world," Adrienne replied, "I thought you would have realised that by now."

"I can't claim to have seen every picture in this city, never mind anywhere else."

Adrienne remembered: "I came across a little gallery the other day, not far from that hotel you like. An English painter. Beautiful colours. You would like them."

"Because the artist is English? You don't know me."

"I couldn't care less where he is from," Adrienne said: "He can paint."

"You mean that I would like them because they are not abstract?"

"You would like them because they are pictures of women without many clothes. Women with big generous boobs."

Giorgio put on a mock stage Irish accent: "What would I be wanting with the likes of them and me a poor man from a far country?"

"I presume that is where you learned the poor mouth."

"It's not just my mouth that does be poor but my pocket as well," Giorgio joked.

Adrienne laughed: "How could you be poor after all the Banks you and your colleagues robbed?"

Giorgio was suddenly seething with anger: "For fuck's sake," he said in a loud whisper as he looked around to see whether people were listening. "Why don't you broadcast it altogether? Put it on radio, television and the Internet."

"I was not thinking." Adrienne bowed her head in shame."

Giorgio's whisper was loud and clear and to the point: "This is what I was afraid of. Loose talk can cost lives."

Neither of them said very much after Adrienne had apologised again. They were inside the gallery at last. There were earphones available through which they could hear a commentary on the paintings in their chosen language. Adrienne made an effort to discuss the Braque and Picasso paintings with Giorgio, but he just pointed to his earpiece as if to say he was hearing all he wabted to hear from rhat source. She knew that he was just sulking and had in mind to just leave him there and walk away if he continued like that. Even the statue of the man with an erection on horseback did not draw a laugh this time.

"Are you going to sulk for the rest of the day?" Adrienne asked when they sat down for a cup of coffee after leaving the gallery.

"What do you mean, sulk?"

"I am sorry that I was not more careful," she said.

"It could be a matter of life or death. I'm sorry that is the way it is, but if we are to go on seeing each other you will need to understand that. I will understand if you don't want to have anything more to do with me."

Adrienne apologised again: "It was a mistake." She reached across the small table and put her hand on his: "Friends," she said.

Giorgio took her hand and looked into her eyes in a very serious manner: "I like you a lot, but I don't want to draw down trouble on you. On either of us for that matter."

Adrienne stood up and siad: "I would like to go back to the apartment right now."

"If that is what you want." Giorgio seemed resigned to the fact that he was going to lose her. "So that's it?"

"Are you stupid or what?" Adrienne asked. "If you don't understand what I have in mind, stay where you are."

Apart from the length of time Adrienne and Giorgio spent kissing on the vaperetto on the way back the rest of the time was spent running. They stopped on the stairs to kiss again, and as soon as they got inside the door they were removing each other's clothes. They ended up on the Persian carpet, naked, wrapped around each other. It was over almost as soon as it started, Giorgio embarrassed at how quickly he came: "I'm sorry. I just could not hold on."

Adrienne kissed him tenderly: "It was just wonderful."

"It was a complete mess. I'm never like that."

"I don't want to know."

He made as if to try and satisfy her with his tongue, but Adrienne said: "Not now, just hold me. Haven't we plenty of time for that? Seize the moment. Enjoy. It's a long time since I felt as I do now."

Giorgio was still embarrassed: "I was in too much of a hurry."

"We both were, but the running and the kissing and the trip in the boat were part of it. It was fantastic."

"You are easy to please."

"Things seldom happen the same way twice," Adrienne said, "but as far as I am concerned that was perfection. Both of us were ready at the same time and we both wanted the same thing."

"You started it," Giorgio smiled. "I thought that you were just about to show me the door."

"Not only did I show you the door, I let you in as well," Adrienne said. "Little did I think when you were sulking in the gallery that we would end up like this, but when I looked over I saw that you looked like a beautiful innocent boy."

"I will have to put on that look as often as I can."

Adrienne kissed him on the lips. She looked into his eyes and said: "I have no idea of what the future holds for us. I am well aware of the difficulties, but I want to be with you more than anyone else at this moment."

Giorgio raised himself on one elbow and looked at Adrienne: "I would like to spend this and every other day making love to you. We should carry on in the way we started."

Adrienne took his hand: "Come on. The bed is more comfortable than the floor." They took things easily when they got there, kissing and hugging, caressing and exploring each other's bodies. Giorgio had no reason to feel embarrassed the next time they completed their lovemaking. He fell asleep in an instant afterwards.

Adrienne held him in her arms for a long time in the centre of the bed. She then got herself into a more comfortable position so that she could watch his face as he slept. She thought of how often she had told Patrick their marriage was over, even though she had not been sure of that in her heart of hearts. She was sure of it now. It was not that she thought Giorgio was suddenly the love of her life, but she was free of the old life. The tie was broken at last."

As she lay looking at her lover, Adrienne remembered that she had completely forgotten about contraception, but that did not worry er in the least. She was ready to welcome a child, even if she had to rear it on her own. All she wanted from the man in her bed at present was friendship and companionship. That was enough, and of course the lovemaking was a bonus.

Adrienne remembered that a year earlier she had been happy enough with her life. Little could she have predicted than that her marriage would have collapsed, another woman would be carrying her husband's child or that she would have started a new life in a city far from home. She was only going to have the one life, and she now intended to live every moment of that life as fully as she could.

Giorgio was snoring, and Adrienne smiled to herself as she gently carressed his body. Herself and Patrick had rarely had sex in the final year of their marriage. She knew now why that was, he was getting enough from Sheila. She was thinking now of having it three times in the one evening. Giorgio was ready to plunge inside her as soon as he awoke

"Where were you for the rest of my life?" he asked as they lay side by side afterwards.

"I was waiting for you, even though I didn't know that you existed."

They slept for most of the evening. About seven o'clock they sent out for a pizza and opened a bottle of wine. They shared the pizza in the bed, feeding each other as in some kind of holy communion. They fell asleep again in the crumbs and leftovers of their meal. Each time they awoke they could not physically get enough of each other.

Giorgio brought coffee and what remained of the pizza to Adrienne as breakfast in bed the following morning.

"Thanks, but coffee will be enough," she said. "Won't you stay with me for the day?"

Giorgio looked at his watch: "They will be sending for me to go to the airport and everywhere."

"Tell them that you are sick, that you are sick with love. On second thoughts leave out the second part, even if it is true."

"I am the complete opposite of being sick," he said. "I never felt so healthy, and I might say that I have proven that in more recent times."

"Tell that crowd at the airport and in the hotel that you are worn out," Adrienne said, "but there is no need to tell them why."

Giorgio seemed anxious: "I need to do at least half a day, or I will be in trouble with the Principe."

"Don't be long because I will be waiting for you." Adrienne sat up in bed to be kissed. "And don't be talking too much to those young Japanese women you were telling me about."

"I will only be thinking of one woman."

By the way, Giorgio, what is your real name?

"I was called Paul at home."

"That is what I am going to call you from now on. It will be our secret." Adrienne blew a kiss as he went out the door.

xviii

GIORGIO RETURNED TO HIS APARTMENT to collect the keys of his water-taxi. The happenings of the previous day and night were so much in his thoughts that he allowed them overide his instincts that something was not right when he put the key in the lock. It just felt different and he had to juggle with it before the door opened. As soon as it opened he got a smell, a people smell that was also for him a smell of danger. It put him on full alert, but it was already too late. The cold barrel of a revolver was placed against the back of his neck by someone hiding behind the door. A tall and burly man emerged from the bathroom. Giorgio noted that he was not carrying a gun, at least in his hands.

"Where is the money?" the man asked casually, as if he was talking about the weather. Giorgio recognised a definite but not very strong Dublin accent. He felt he would be dead already if it was an assasin sent by the movement. "Druggies," he thought. He had even more enemies in that quarter.

He answered in Italian, speaking as quickly as he could to try and confuse his assailants as much as possible.

"OK, so you've learned the language. Good man. I hope you need it where you are going," the big man said. "You didn't answer my question, by the way, unless you did so with that mumbo jumbo. Where is the money?"

Giorgio answered with another question, in English this time: "What money are you talking about?"

"There is no need to be shy with us," the man said, as if chatting to a friend. "We know all about you."

"The only money I have is from taxi fares," Giorgio answered. "It's not much but you can have it." He emptied out his pockets.

"I would hate to have to beat it out of you." The big man made a fist with his right hand and looked down at it, as if it would pain himself more than Giorgio if he had to use it. At the same time the person behind him pushed the gun into his neck.

Giorgio gestured over his shoulder and asked the man in front of him: "Is it a woman that is behind me, or a man that wears perfume?"

The big fellow studied his fist again and shook his head as if more in sorrow than in anger: "You are looking for a good hiding."

You've got it wrong there," Giorgio said. "In fact I am looking to find out what you are doing in my apartment." He felt there was a chance of surviving this as long as they thought that he had a stash of money somewhere. It would be of no use to them if they killed him. For the first time in his life really he was getting to use the volunteer training he had endured in caves and mountain sides when he had joined up with the paramilitaries at first. The mantra: "Don't give any information you don't need to" was part of that training.

"You've obviously got the wrong man. I have no idea what money you are talking about."

The big man came forward and gave him a gentle slap in the face: "The next one will be a lot harder if you don't spill the beans. Where have you put our money?"

"I never stole from anyone in my life," Giorgio said. "I'm no saint, but I am not a thief either."

"Think, think . . ." the big man slapped him on both cheeks in a quick and intimate kind of way. "What did you do with the Major's money? Where did you hide the million?"

Giorgio knew who the Major was, a drugs baron given that name by the press in the same way as Martin Cahill had been called 'The General.' It had been his pleasure to take out the Major with a single bullet in the side of the head from a hundred metres as he sat in his car in a Dublin suburb. He had been shocked when asked to do the job at first, as he thought the 'Major' in question was the then British Prime Minister, John Major. He was aware from the tabloid press who the real 'Major' was. He had studied his movements for a fortnight before blowing off the top of his head with a dumdum bullet.

"I was never within a hundred yards of the Major," he answered truthfully.

"He was taken out with a long shot," the big man acknowledged. "But then his money was taken from the car."

At this stage Giorgio felt there was little point in denying the shooting: "I was out of there as quickly as I could. I was not anywhere near the car, and that's the honest truth."

"Where did his money go if you didn't take it?"

Giorgio did not have a clue: "I did not even know that he was carrying any money."

The girl behind him spoke for the first time: "The money was in the car, ready for a deal, a million of the old money."

"Sandra would know," the big man said. "She is the Major's daughter and she is just looking for her inheritance."

"All this happened years ago," Giorgio said. "Why are you only searching for it now."

"Because the man who fired the shot was conveniently dead," the big man said. "dead and buried and gone to heaven," we all thought, "but like all great guys he rose again on the third day."

"What made you think I was here?"

"A little birdie was on the way from the airport with a wad of coke. He thought the boat driver looked like that second rate Che Guevara who was a bit of a pin-up the time he got the military funeral"

"You have a good line in sarcasm," Giorgio said to the man.

"You're not too bad yourself," he replied.

"So you have come for your pound of flesh?" Giorgio asked, anything to keep talking, the best hope of any hostage.

"There is at least a hundredweight of flesh to be garnered in this instance," was the big man's view. "It's just normal family stuff really. A girl wants what is left to her in her father's will. A million pounds. What is that in euros? Allow for inflation, Cost of collection, etc, etc. A couple of million should cover it."

"So she is out for revenge?" Giorgio asked.

"Give us our money and we are out the door," Sandra said.

"And you will just let me walk away, I suppose?" Giorgio sounded as if he had serious doubts about that.

"We will cut you a deal if you give us the money," the man said.

"You have not a shred of evidence that I took any money. Would I be living in a rundown apartment like this if I was rich? If this was a court of law you wouldn't have a leg to stand on."

Sandra answered that one: "If this was a court of law you wouldn't have us as judge and jury."

"Not to speak of executioner," Giorgio said ruefully.

"You are hardly trying to tell us that it was the pigs that took it," the big man said. "The squad was the first car on the scene. I wouldn't put it past them, but they wouldn't be smart enough to get away with it."

"Maybe some little gurrier came along before the Guards arrived," Giorgio suggested.

He got a suden blow to the face. Blood spurted from Giorgio's mouth and ran down his face. "This will stop when you tell us where the money is," the big man said in a sympathetic voice, like a doctor gently counselling a patient.

The gun bedind Giorgio's head shook: "Do you remember how you blew off my Da's head? It will give me great satisfaction to do the same to you. I have got similar bullets."

"So much for cutting a deal," was Giorgio's reply. "Go on, get it over, and you can search Venice for your money. If you want a deal you will have to let me go when you get money."

"Now you're talking." The man said. "A minute ago you were telling us that you didn't take anything from the Major's car."

"It's not the same money. It's the money I got as a payoff from the movement when they faked my death. It's supposed to be my pension, but it won't be much good to me if I'm dead."

"How much?" Sandra asked.

"Where is it?" was her companion's question

"A quarter of a million or so."

The big man spoke as if he was the most patient person in the world, but he slapped Giorgio across the face at the same time: "Where is it?"

"I'm hardly going to tell you if you keep treating me like that."

The man stepped back from him: "Point made, Now where is it?"

"I will have to bring you out in my boat," Giorgio began to explain.

The man laughed: "Oh, yeah, The Dogger Bank. I know that one."

Sandra asked: "What do you mean, out in a boat?"

"You hardly think I have it lodged in the Bank of Venice. I have it hidden in a lobster pot out on the water. You wouldn't find a safer place, much safer than on land."

"It is probably soaked in water and half-rotten," Sandra suggested.

"It is as well wrapped as those bales of drugs that you import," Giorgio told her. There is no water getting in there."

"Where is your boat?" the man asked.

"She is tied down outside the door. It's a speedboat, as safe as could be. You could turn it over and it would right itself again."

"Let's go," Sandra said.

Giorgio indicated the blood on his face: "There will be reports to the Carbineri if I appear outside like this."

"Watch out for tricks," Sandra told her companion. He poured water from the kettle into a basin. He splashed this on Giorgio's face and handed him a tea towel to dry it off."

"There is blood on my shirt as well," Giorgio said. Sandra took another shirt from the back of the chair and threw it at him: "Put that on."

"That's for the wash," Giorgio said. "It's all sweaty."

"Don't worry about it," she half giggled: "We won't be getting near enough to you to smell you." He saw her for the first time as he was putting on the shirt. She was tall and fairly goodlooking with short blonde-dyed hair. She was dressed more like a Bank teller than what he would imagine as a gangster's moll. She put her revolver in her bag while still holding the handle and trigger and waved him towards the door. The man could not resist kicking him in the backside: "No funny stuff. If this is some kind of a trick, you will pay dearly for it."

"Hold on a minute," Giorgio said when they reached the top of the stairs. Sandra raised her handbag with the gun immediately:
"What is it?"

"You would be better to wait until after dark."

The big man asked why and Giorgio explained that they were hardly going to get in the boat together without thousands of eye-witnesses, tourist and local alike. "There will ba lots of suspicions if my body is found out in the lagoon."

"You won't be left out there," the man said. "We will need you to drive the boat back."

"So you won't kill me until then?"

"Let's go," the man said, "and get this over."

The woman was not so sure. She asked Giorgio: "Is it safer after dark?"

He answered that it was safer in the sense that there would not be eye-witnesses. "You do want to get back to Dublin before they find my body?"

"It's a long day to be hanging around," Sandra said.

Giorgio could not resist a sarcastic dig: "You could go and see a couple of art galleries or some of the paintings in the churches. I'll mind the house while you are gone."

The man shut his mouth with a punch which suggested that he had been a boxer. He told Sandra to keep the gun on Giorgio while he was finding something with which to tie him up. He pulled the belt from a dressing gown and tied his hands with one end and his feet with the other. He then left him lying on his side in a very uncomfortable position.

"If you feel like tea or coffee," Giorgio said, "don't hesitate. What's mine is yours in every sense of the word." He and his republican colleagues had been taught during training to keep talking in such a situation, even though he did not quite understand why. "Even if you are badly beaten, keep talking," they had been told. It had something to do with confusing their captors or keeping them from focusing properly on their plans. If it was possible to build up any kind of a relationship, they had been told to do so. Having a human relationship, however fractious made it harder for people to kill their victims according to those theories.

Giorgio's attempts at conversation and sarcasm were studiously ignored by his captors. They did take him up on the offer to have something to eat and drink. Sandra prepared coffee and took bread, butter and cheese from his fridge. They spoke to each other in low voices, and in so far as he could make out, Giorgio was pleased to note that they did not seem to be in complete agreement.

As he lay tied up in his bed, Giorgio remembered the last bed he had lain in and the pleasure he and Adrienne had shared. He felt that there must still be remnants of catholic guilt inside him, that he was paying in some way for the previous day's pleasure. Whatever about that Adrienne was now the main reason he wanted to survive his present predicament.

He was still thinking of Adrienne when the mobile phone in his pocket began to ring. The big man came over and took it away. The ringing stopped and then started again. The man threw the phone on the floor and squashed it with his heel.

"You won't be calling anyone on that anytime soon," he said.

"It would not have been easy to answer it with my hands tied," Giorgio said even though he sensed it would lead to further beating. His instincts were right and his nose was soon bleeding again.

"Do it again," Giorgio encouraged him. "I like to meet a man that is into sado-machicism."

He got another slap: "Shut your dirty mouth. There is a woman in the company."

"There are two," Giorgio answered him.

The big man raised his right fist: "What do you mean by that?"

"A real man would not hit someone lying tied and helpless on a bed. For that matter a real woman wouldn't either."

"I'll do what I like." The man kicked him as well as he could, given that Giorgio was on the bed. "If you don't like the feel of my hands, I'll let you have taste of my feet instead."

Giorgio teased: "What a brave bully you are."

Sandra came over with lighted cigarettes for herself and her companion. "Don't overdo it," she said. "We still need him to get the money for us when it gets dark."

The man put his cigarette within half an inch of Giorgio's eyes: "Only for we need you to get us the money your lovely little eyes would be toast. He then burnt his eyebrows with the cigarrette.

Sandra seemed to be getting worried that he would go over the top. She led him over to the table and they talked together in low voices.

Giorgio kept up the pressure: "Feel free to go up on each other or whatever ye do for fun," he shouted across the room.

The man came running over and gave him a kick in the ribs: "Shut your mouth or I will shut it for you."

Sandra came and took his arm: "Take no heed of him. Can't you see he is trying to wind us up. He is trying to mess with our heads."

"I'll mess with his head," the man said angrily. "My boot will mess with his bollocks if he says anything like that again."

"Have I hit a sore spot?" Giorgio asked. "Is it how you're not able to get it up? Poor Sandra isn't getting her oats." The man was rising from his chair but Sandra pushed him back: "Don't let him get to you."

"He is insulting you. He is insulting both of us," her companion said: "He can insult all he likes. We will have our money and he will be dead before the night is out."

"Ye can sing for your money," Giorgio said. "I'm hardly going to show you where it is and then let you kill me."

"I was just exaggerating," Sandra said. "All I am really interested in is the money."

"To buy more drugs?" Giorgio asked.

"Ignore him," Sandra told her colleague and they didn't answer that or any other question from Giorgio."

"Am I talking to myself?" he asked after some time. "Do ye not love me anymore? After eating my breakfast and everything."

No reply. The other two talked between themselves. They seemed to be agreeing with each other at this stage. He tried to think os something that would elicit a response from them.

After a while he said loudly: "I hope the money is where I left it."

No response from across the room.

"I hope that it has not been eaten by crabs or worms."

"Don't rise to the bait," Sandra told her mate.

"Good pun, Sandra," Giorgio said. Worms, bait and all that."

The big man approached: "Are you trying to insult the daughter of a man you murdered."

"It was justice," Giorgio said. "Rough justice, but justice all the same."

The man put a closed fist to Giorgio's face: I am in the humour to beat the shit out of you."

"Get on with it. Just kill me. Isn't that what you intend to do anyway. What have I to lose? I don't know will I bother telling you where the money is. It depends on what humour I'm in."

Sandra tried to reassure him: "I guarantee that we will let you go if you get us the money."

"And what Bank will I change that guaranttee in?" Giorgio asked.

"I swear on my father's grave."

Although she was not facing him Giorgio sensed her lack of sincerity: "Why did you wink at your man while you were saying it?"

"How do you know?" She had said it before she thought of herself.

"Did you ever hear of hindsight? That means having an eye in your backside. I don't miss anything. You don't need an extra eye to detect lies and deceit."

"Get us the money," she said, "and we will see."

Giorgio tried to wind them up again: "I understand why you hate me, Sandra, because I killed your father, but Gozilla, the gorilla here. I don't see what he has against me."

This angered the big man. He raised a fist: "Who are you calling a gorilla. I'll give you gorilla." Sandra took his arm before he had time to hit Giorgio: "Can't you see that is what he wants. Don't open your mouth to him from now until evening." She shouted across to Giorgio:

"What time do you intend to take us out in the boat?"

"At nightfall. Twilght, when nobody out there will recognise anyone or anything."

Sandra was suspicious: "Will it not be too dark to find the money then?"

Giorgio felt the answer came to him from nowhere: "I have it marked on the radar," he said, fairly sure they knew little about that technology. "It will guide us to the very spot." He remembered an Irish language story from school about a Kerry boy called "Jimín Mháire Thaidhg." Having found a good fishing ground, he put a mark on the seat of the boat with his penknife, thinking that would help him find that place again.

xix

ADRIENNE FELT A MIXTURE OF anger and worry as the day went on. Giorgio, or Paul as she thought of him now, had not returned early as he had promised and his mobile phone seemed to be switched off. It was not even accepting her messages or texts. She had rarely felt so happy and contented as when she awoke in the middle of the day, thinking that her lover would soon be home. One o'clock, two, three and four came and went. She got up, had coffee, had a shower, dressed, thinking that he would call on the intercom at any minute, asking her to open the apartment door. She stood out on the balcony and peeed down to see was his water-taxi at the bottom of the steps. There was no sight of it there. She scanned the canal but it was not within sight there either. It was then that she considered for the first time that he might not be coming back.

"Men," she said angrily to herself. "Why does any woman trust any of them?"

Whoever was the first woman to say that men were only interested in one thing was right, she thought. That got what they wanted, they went hunting for the next woman. They were all the same, Patrick, Giorgio, Paul or whatever this fellow was called. She knew the name that she would call him. She herself had not been intimate with many men, but from what she had heard about them generally they were all the same. Hunters As soon as they captured their prey they were on the lookout again. It was all about the chase, They knew nothing of loyalty or fidelity.

"If we had a fight or something it would be different," Adrienne told herself. But after such a lovely evening." Then the thought struck: "I hope that nothing has happened to him."

For the first time that evening Adrienne's anger was replaced by worry, a deep feeling in the pit of her stomach that Giorgio was in some kind of trouble. That would explain why he had not returned. She had never really trusted boats and water, and then there were his fears that he was being followed, that he was in danger, that both of them could be in danger. Should she ring the police? He would not be too impressed if she did and it turned out that he had to do a few extra fares. But why couldn't he ring her or even text? A couple of words on a mobile was not going to wear out his thumb. She could not wait for him to return. She looked from the balcony again, knowing full well that she was probably wasting her time.

"Why don't I have dinner ready for him when he comes back?" Adrienne asked herself. She thought of the implications. Would this give the impression that it was alright to wander in at any time of the day or night, even if someone had arranged a time? Would she be signalling that she was an oldfashioned traditional woman who had dinner on the table for her man every evening even if he had not the manners to phone or text? She rubbished such thoughts: "It's not as if we are married or committed. We only got together yesterday. Won't I need a bite to eat mself as well?" She took her shopping bag and headed out of the apartment.

Adrienne had in mind to buy fresh fish in the local market, but decided to go to Hotel Principe first. She knew that Giorgio got much of his business from there, and they would probably be able to trace him on their network. She felt that thee would be simple explanation for his absence, a long journey maybe to an area that had no mobile phone coverage. She hopped on a vaperetto that would bring her close to the hotel

Patrick rang while she was on the boat:

"What is it?" she asked sharply. She felt she had enough on her mind without having to console her former husband.

Patrick seemed to be in high good humour: "And how are you in the city of love and romance?"

Adrienne guessed the reason for his humour: "Sheila had the baby?"

"How do you know?"

"Because you sound like a little boy with a new toy. Is it a boy or a girl?"

"A boy, I'm told, even though I have only seen his face so far."

Adrienne tried to put heart into her "Congratulations" even though her emotions were mixed. She told herself to be strong, that he was no longer her husband, that life was over, but it was not easy.

Patrick didn't seem to notice: "Thank you," he said. "I really am grateful."

"Grateful for what?" Adrienne asked.

"For your good wishes. It can't be easy for you. I thought you should hear it from me rather than from someone else."

"There are not too many around here who would be minding my business for me, like thay would at home," she said. "I don't think it would be the top of the list of topics from the baker or pizza maker."

"Your friends from home might be calling you."

"None of them would want to be first with that story," Adrienne said. "They know how I feel."

"I know that it hurts you, that I have hurt you," Patrick said.

"I couldn't give a damn either way," Adrienne spoke as lightly as she could to hide her hurt. That is all in the past. I am actually sailing through the centre of Venice in a boat just now, with the sun shining, and without a care in the world."

Patrick was still being defensive: "I never thought when it started . . ."

Adrienne interrupted: "Is Sheila alright?"

"She is fine. Tired, of course, and the baby will be kept in for a while because it is premature, but he will be improving by the day with the help of God."

"I see you have found Jesus along the way," Adrienne said.

"I wouldn't go that far," Patrick answered, "but you would want the best for the little mite."

"Of course you would." Adrienne finished their conversation abruptly by saying she had to get off the boat and she needed the use of both hands. This was only half true, but she was soon on shore and heading for the hotel.

The tall thin man at the desk in the Principe did not give her much information. He had not seen or heard from Giorgio since morning. There had been no water-taxi needed. "Vaperetto, vaperetto," he said as he gestured with both hands, letting her know that was how that day's tourists had travelled. She wondered why a hotel which dealt constantly with tourists would have a man at the desk who had so little English.

Jonny at the bar shook his head and said he had not seen Giorgio for a couple of days. He gave the impression that she was not the only woman to look for him. "Giorgio many woman, much love," he said with a big smile.

Adrienne accepted from that that she was unlikely to see Giorgio again except by accident. It was obviously not a bullet that had taken him out of commission but Cupid's arrow. "How do I know that it is not at home with his wife and family he is?" she said to herself. "Everything he told me was probably a pack of lies." She still had a lingering feeling that he was in some kind of trouble.

Adrienne went to the market. She wondered was Monday the best day to look for fresh fish in Italy or anywhere else. She bought prawns and escallopes, wondering were they really fresh or had they been defrosted. The fishmonger was of little help. Either he did not understand her or conveniently pretended that he could not. He had his hands in the air as he spoke at speed as if he and his produce had been insulted by her temerity in asking a question. The girl in the wine stall understood her a little better, white wine that was dry but not like vinegar. She said that a particular wine would complement the fish she had bought, and winked before saying her partner should like it too.

Adrienne felt better having spoken to someone who was kind and who understood her. The other man probably treated everyone like that, and women especially, but when you were in a strange country trying to converse in a foreign tongue, a litle kindness went a long way. "For all I know Paul might be home before me," she thought, "and all this worry will have been a waste of time." She really had no reason not to be positive. The simplest of things might have delayed him, an engine breakdown on the way from the airport maybe. "I don't own him," she told herself. "He is entitled to do anything he likes."

"Paul!" Adrienne called his name as she opened the door of her apartment. She had not given him a key but she hoped the caretaker might have let him in. She realised that she had been expecting too much. Like other setbacks in her life, she felt that she would just have to put this behind her and get back to painting. That was what she did after she separated from Patrick. That was what kept her sane. It should be a lot easier to forget this one-night stand than her husband of ten years.

Adrienne used the darkest colours she had to express her mood, but put a bright spot in the top right hand corner to denote the sun. It would show that she was disappointed but not without hope. She stood back to assess the small picture she had painted in less than an hour. Those who thought it crazy to charge a thousand euro for an hours work were wrong, she thought. There was more to it than the time it took to paint. There was the darkness of life brightened by a small touch of hope. And there were many days in which she did not earn a cent. Right now money was of little interest. Her pain had been eased by her work, but it had not gone away.

Adrienne cleaned the one brush she had used in case it would accidentally touch the picture and change it in any way. It seemed as good as anything she had ever painted. The ability to transfer her feelings to the canvas astounded her. Like creativity itself it was something that she could not understand. No feeling, no pain was ever wasted because she could use it in her art. Paul or Giorgio or whatever he called himself was probably sailing around thinking of the great time he had with that vulnerable woman. The poor fool did not know that his rejection had earned her a thousand euro. She would be the one to have the last laugh, even though she would much prefer to have his company instead.

XX

Night was falling when the big man cut the belt of the dressinggown with which he had tied Giorgio. The evening had passed quickly as he had slept because his captors had gone quiet. The training he had received for such an eventuality but never had to use until now had worked. They had been told to grab any sleep they could. That would give them an advantage over hostage takers who had to stay awake to see that there was no danger of their hostages escaping.

Despite having little enough sleep the night before as well as the battering from the big man, Giorgio felt alert when he awoke. He was stiff and sore after being tied in an awkward position for so long. He did not like to be in the situation in which he was, but he felt he still had a chance. When your back is to the wall the only thing to do is come out fighting. Fighting with brain as well as brawn. The clearest advantage he had was that they needed him to get this mythical money, but they seemed to know nothing about boats.

As soon as he was awake, Giorgio began to tease his captors, and especially the big man again: "It's a long time since I slept so well in a bed on my own. I enjoyed being tied up. I often wondered what was the big deal, why do some people like ropes and whips. Do ye use them yourselves?"

"Shut your dirty mouth," the man ordered. "Or I will close it for you."

Giorgio looked around: "Is there an echo in this place? I thought I heard those words earlier. I think there might have been a gorilla screeching in the trees."

He got a kick in the backside for his trouble: "Keep talking like that and your chanches of living are getting slimmer by the minute."

"I didn't think I had a chance at all," Giorgio said.

"If it wasn't for the money you would be swimming with the fishes already," Sandra said. "To pay for my father's death."

"I think you were watching to many gangster movied," Giorgio replied "Which family do you resemble most, the Corleones or the Sopranos?"

The man caught Giorgio by the shoulder: "Enough of your old guff. Get going towards the boat."

They left the apartment in the same way as before, Sandra with the gun in her handbag ready to fire if necessary, the man guiding Giorgio by the shoulder. He put his hand across both shoulders when they met someone on the stairs, partly to make space and partly to pretend they were old friends going out for the evening.

"I am not trying to trick you when I say this," Giorgio said as they neared the bottom of the second flight of stairs. "It is important."

Sandra told him to spit it out.

"One of you will have to pull up the rope attached to the pot when we get to where the money is. I won't be able to control the boat with the wheel and pull in the pot at the same time."

The man displayed a complete ignorance of the sea or fishing: "What kind of an effing pot are you talking about?"

"The pot of gold," Giorgio said. "A lobster pot really, a kind of a basket with a bit of ballast at the bottom. It's heavy enough so it will take a strong man to pull it in out of the sea."

The girl raised the handbag with the gun: "I smell a rat here."

"Do you want your money or not?" Giorgio asked. "All I am saying is that I can't do this on my own. You will have to help me."

"If you make one false move . . ." Sandra did not need to finish her sentence.

"You can keep me covered with that thing, and let him pull in the pot," Giorgio suggested. They had reached the boat at this stage and he told them to put on their jackets. He indicated the box with the lifjackets.

The man was suspicious: "Why?"

"Do you want to get drowned?" Giorgio asked him.

"If there is anyone getting drowned it will be you," came the reply.

"You are going to need your jackets so. You may have to swim back if you don't know how to handle the boat."

They looked at each other as if not sure what to do. They then ordered him to get them a jacket each from the box. On the pretence that he was trying to get ones the right size he picked two which did not carry the name of the boat. They took a jacket each and put it on, taking turns to keep Giorgio covered with the revolver while doing so. They did not allow Giorgio to put on a jacket, as they seemed to think he would be less likely to dive into the sea in order to escape, without one.

Giorgio drove his boat slowly and carefully by the vaperettos and gondolas towards the mouth of the harbour. He kept the lights on the boat dimmed at the suggestion of his captors so that they would not be recognisable, or that nobody would know how many passengers he carried.

He looked at the big familiar buildings and the bridges as if they were old friends he might be meeting for the last time. He felt confident that he had the upper hand on the two in the boat with him, but they might turn out to be smarter than he thought. Anything could happen when there was a revolver ready to be fired in the company.

The biggest advantage Giorgio felt that he had was that the others seemed unable to handle the boat, and he hoped that they would not be stupid enough to try and do so. As far as he could see they had no plan except to get their hands on the money and then get rid of him. They lacked the professionalism of other drug gangs he had observed. The best thing he could do was to concentrate on his own plan but at the same time to be ready for anything untoward that happened.

Giorgio suddenly let out the throttle as soon as they reached the open sea. The water-taxi began to bounce off small waves with considerable noise. His passengers lost their feet and were soon scrambling to steady themselves. The big man was roaring to slow down, while Giorgio pretended not to be able to hear him above the noise of the engine and the boat bouncing on the waves. "What?" he shouted back, every time the man roared at him. The man took the gun from Sandra and put it to Giorgio's ear with some force: "Slow fucking down or I will blow your head off."

Giorgio did what he was told more in fear that the gun would be set off by the hopping of the boat than anything. The boat was now rising and falling with the waves without any control because the engine was cut off.

"That's the way it is at sea," Giorgio said. "It's not my fault. You can see yourselves that the waves are there. That's nature."

"You don't need to go so fast?" the man said.

"That is what speedboats do," was Giorgio's reply.

"Don't get smart with me."

"I'll go a bit slower, but be prepared for a long night on the water."

The man addressed Giorgio in a more civil way than he had done for a long time: How long is it going to take to get to the money?"

"At least an hour if we are going slower." Giorgio wanted to get them out as far as possible before getting them overboard if he could manage to do so. The further out they were the better chance of bodies being carried by the tides to the other side of the Adriatic.

"We are not in a hurry," Sandra said. "Whatever time it takes to get the money. Have you enough diesel?""

"I filled her yesterday."

"Move," the man ordered, "but not too quick."

"I can't go too slow," Giorgio explained, "or it will be like one step forward and two steps back. We are against wind and tide. If I don't give it a bit of throttle we will get nowhere."

"Let's go," Sandra said. Giorgio went forward at the same speed as he had used earlier, and it was not long before the big man was seasick in the cabin.

"You should have put it out over the side," Giorgio said angrily. "I will have a big clean-up to do before I can carry any passengers. The smell of puke will linger for a week."

"A pity about you," the man answered, wiping his mouth with the sleeve of his jacket. Giorgio thought he was gaining psychological advantage as the man was as pale as death.

"Seasickness is contagious," Giorgio shouted to Sandra in the cabin, especially when you are in where the vomit is."

She stood out and hung on to the rail beside him with one hand, the gun in the other. She was not wearing gloves and he was aware that her hands would be freezing. His paramilitary trainers had taught him that it was important to note every possible advantage.

"Any chance of you?" Giorgio shouted to Sandra above the sound of the engine. He had noticed the man being sick again in the cabin, and he himself was using every method possible to rile the girl beside him.

"What?" she asked as if she couldn't believe her ears.

"Would the ride be out of the question? When we get rid of your man."

Sandra was obviously becoming extremely angry: "If you were the last man in the world . . ."

"If you were the last woman we wouldn't have much choice but to get it on. To save the planet."

"You actually deserve to die," Sandra said. "You kill my father and now you treat me like dirt."

"Over there," Giorgio pointed.

Sandra's eyes followed the line of his hand: "What's over there?"

"The money."

"Where?"

"Do you see the white buoy?"

"Where exactly? As she turned away slightly Giorgio opened the throttle and pushed her in the back at the same time. She went over the side of the boat as if she was a gymnast doing a cartwheel."

The big man heard her screech and hurried unsteadily from the cabin: "Where is Sandra?" he asked, confused.

Giorgio pointed; "She felt like a swim." He suddenly wheeled the boat to starboard which had the effect of catapulting the man who had no grip on anything out over the side.

Giorgio straightened up the boat which came close to capsizing with the sudden turn and the speed. He could hardly believe his luck in getting rid of his captors so easily. He turned the boat in a wide circle and headed for the lights of Venice. He did not look back. He sent no SOS or MAYDAY signal. It had been them or him, death or life They had tried to mess with the wrong man.

On the return journey Giorgio hauled in a few buckets of water and cleaned out the cabin as best he could. He was feeling the effect of the beating the big man had meted out and found it hard to do anything except drive the boat back home. He had not forgotten his meticulous training. He used chemicals to remove any DNA evidence when he got back and tied up his water-taxi. The apartment would need cleaning too, but that was a job for the following day. Right now all he wanted to do was to see Adrienne again. He took the vaperetto as closely as he could to her apartment, and staggered the rest of the way.

xxi

Aᴅʀɪᴇɴɴᴇ ᴡᴀꜱ ɢᴇᴛᴛɪɴɢ ʀᴇᴀᴅʏ ᴛᴏ go to bed when the intercom bell rang. She asked who it was and was told: "Paul."

"Where are you going at this time of the night?" she asked. She had spent the evening and night trying to deal with his disappearance, and now that she had convinced herself that she would never see him again, here he was. She could feel the anger build up inside her.

"I wanted to see you," he answered. Adrienne thought he was drunk when she heard his voice which seemed more gutteral than previously.

"You can't just turn up here anytime you like," Adrienne told him. "Where were you all day? You promised that you would be here in the afternoon."

"It's a long story," he said. "Please let me in and I will tell you."

"It's a story I don't particularly want to hear right now. Come back if you want when you ae sober."

"I haven't been drinking. The last drink I had was when I was here with you. You don't need to listen to my story if you want. Just help me please. I've been beaten up badly."

Adrienne pressed the button: "Come up," she said. She got a shock when she saw the dried blood on his face as well as other cuts and bruises. "What happened?"

He told his story in dribs and drabs as he lay in the bath while Adrienne gently tended to his wounds. He groaned in pain when she touched his side. "I think I may have broken ribs."

"I'll call a doctor."

"No doctor. I've broken some before playing football. Three weeks or so and they will be right as rain."

"You just left them there to die in the sea?" Adrienne asked when told about Sandra and her companion.

Paul had no pity for them: "They had lifejackets."

"You know they have no chance of survival?"

"It was them or me, life or death."

"Murder," she said.

130

"Self defence. Would you prefer if they had killed me?"

"You know I wouldn't." Adrienne tried to kiss him, but that hurt his lips. She still was not happy with abandoning people at sea: "Even in a war the Red Cross would be allowed to pick up the wounded."

"I was the wounded," was Paul's answer to that. "Do you think they would have called the Red Cross for me?"

"You are the one who is supposed to be civilised."

"What makes you think that? I have spent much of my life as a soldier, not a soldier of the State, but a soldier all the same. I don't have the usual liberal sensibilities. I would not be alive now if I had. What choice have I but to defend myself if someone attacks me?"

"I suppose," Adrienne said, but it was clear that she was uncomfortable with the concept. They left it at that. Paul fell asleep quickly after taking painkillers she had for her period, his ribs bound with some of Adrienne's scarves. She sat for some time, watching him sleep, deep and troubling thoughts running through her mind.

Adrienne asked herself was it for this she had left Patrick and started a new life far from home. She was sinking deeper and deeper into trouble since she met this man, attractive and all as he was. It was not just that he acknowledged that he had killed people while in the movement, but in the last few hours he had left two to die without mercy in the cold of the Adriatic. She was as guilty as he was, morally and legally because she was now sheltering him. She could spend the rest of her life in prison. What was she supposed to do about it now that he was there sleeping in her bed? Life with Patrick might have been fairly boring, but this was the complete opposite.

She lay into the bed beside Paul after midnight, careful not to touch his ribs or other areas that hurt. For some reason she thought of Sheila on her maternity bed, her child in an incubator nearby. How life had changed. Still she too might have a baby some day. Maybe one of the many seed that had entered her body the previous day might be sailing close to one of her eggs at this very moment. If it was to happen that a child was created with this man who was hard enough to abandon two human beings to the sea, what kind of person would that child turn out to be? Would she want to have such a child? Right now she felt she would welcome any child.

Paul awoke sometime during the night, confused and sore. Adrienne had to help him to the bathroom and hold her arm around his shoulders while he urinated. He apologised for the lack of dignity involved.

"Don't worry about it," she said. "I am as deep in this at this stage as you are."

She brought him breakfast in the morning and he managed to eat porridge, spooned to him like feeding a child, because his lips were so sore.

"Turn on the radio," he said, "to see is there any news about last night."

It took Adrienne some time to find a local station, as her radio had been tuned into news from home. She did not understand much of the news that came in the headlines at the top of the next hour. Paul seemed satisfied: "There was nothing about those two. The bodies must have been washed out to sea."

"Are you sure it's bodies? They had lifejackets."

Paul had no doubt: "It's bodies if they were out there all night."

Adrienne shook her head but did not say anything.

"Don't expect me to be sorry for them. It was them or me, the survival of the fittest, the law of the jungle."

"They could be after you again tomorrow," Adrenne said.

"I doubt it. Even if they were lucky enough to be picked up by a fishing boat, I imagine they have learned their lesson. They picked on the wrong man."

"There will be some kind of an enquiry if they are found, dead or alive," Adrienne said.

"It will look like they fell off a cruise ship or a yacht, maybe, or of one of those refugee boats if their bodies are washed ashore, or found in somebody's fishing net."

"There is DNA and all kinds of forensics nowadays."

Paul had his own view on that: "I can tell you straight up that the authorities will be happier to find them dead than alive. There will be two drugdealers less on the streets."

"The law is there to protect the criminal as well as the so-called civilised person."

"Surely you are not naïve enough to believe that," Paul said. "Do you think that those in charge back home did not rejoice every time some poor unfortunate in the IRA blew himself up accidentally? Do you think they were not delighted at my supposed death? The same is true of drug barons. A good clean killing saves all the courts and the law and the solicitors an awful lot of bother. Nothing pleases the authorities more than to see them killing each other. It is the most logical thing in the world. Every enemy taken out is one enemy less to deal with."

"That is an awfully cynical attitude," Adrienne commented.

"A very realistic attitude." They agreed to differ by not discussing the matter any further.

Adsrienne helped Paul to sit watching television and then began to prepare her canvas and brushes."

"Why are you looking at me like that?" Paul asked a short while later.

"I would like to paint your portrait. Nobody will get to see it except yourself, or with your permission."

"You want to paint me battered and bruised?" he asked.

"You remind me of pictures of the crucified Christ."

Paul burst out laughing but had to put his hands to his mouth as his broken lips hurt: "That is the first time I have been compared with your man, Jesus."

"Some of the finest art in the world is based on his passion," Adrienne said. "Would you be willing to sit there and let me paint you? You can still be watching the television."

"The last thing I want is to be recognised," Paul answered, but I probably wont be in the kind of pictures that you paint. I presume this is going to be abstract?"

"It's the only kind that I do, and you can burn it if you don't like it," she told him.

"You can hardly make me any worse than I look at the moment."

"Just wait and see."

Adrienne did not allow Paul to see the painting while she worked. From time to time she looked carefully at him from one angle or another, and then returned to the canvas. He became absorbed in an Italian soap-opera and lost count of time. Then Adrienne turned the canvas towards him and asked: "Well, what do you think?"

"That is supposed to be me?"

Adrienne shrugged: "A picture of wounded humanity."

"For a moment I thought you were going to say wounded innocence."

"That might be pushing it."

"There is certainly plenty of blood in it," Paul said, "if that is what the deep red is supposed to signify."

"It is not meant to be realistic."

"Symbolic so?" Paul asked.

Adrienne put her head slightly to one side as she often did when considering something: "There is some of that there, but there is also strength and courage and pain, and not a little cruelty."

"Cruelty?" Paul asked as if that word hurt him.

"I thought what you did yesterday was very cruel, not to speak of what you told me about yourself the other day."

"I had to do those things."

"That's what the Nazis said at Nuremberg," Adrienne answered. "They were under orders."

"Are you calling me a Nazi now? I haven't gassed any Jews so far," Paul answered sarcastically

"You know that is not what I am saying."

"Well what are you saying?" Paul seemed to be getting angry.

Adrienne spoke slowly, as she strove for the right words: "I understand to some extent what you did yesterday, especially as your life was in danger. To tell you the truth I don't know which would be more cruel, to kill those two on the spot, or to leave them to die in the water as you did."

"I did leave them with a chance. They had lifejackets. I didn't kill them. They might be on board some ship drinking rum right now."

Adrienne's look told that she thought this was very far-fetched.

"What happened yesterday will always come between us?"

"It doesn't have to," Adrienne said. "If it had really come between us that much, you would hardly be here. I am doing my level best to understand you. Help me, please."

"What can I say?"

"Would you kll me?" Adrienne asked.

"If I had to," Paul replied.

Adrienne drew a deep breath: "I know where I stand now. Why would you have to kill me?"

"If you wre pointing a gun at me and were likely to fire. The same as yesterday. Self defence."

Adrienne had to smile, almost in spite of herself: "I am hardly likely to shoot you with a paintbrush."

"This time yesterday a woman had a gun behind my ear," Paul said. "I did not want to kill her, but what choice had I? She still had a gun in her hand when I got her overboard."

"Did she fall or was she pushed?"

"If she had not fallen she would have been pushed, or I would have been shot. As I have said many times already, what choice had I?"

Adrienne did not try to answer that question She had a thousand answers in her mind but it was not her that was in his position, being beaten and threatened. She concentrated on what was practical:

"Do you need to make arrangements about your boat, or tell someone that your taxi will not be available for a while?"

"Could you write me a notice on the computer to put up in the Principe hotel?" he asked.

Adrienne made a mock bow like a ham actor: "Your wish is my command, sir. No sooner said than done." When she had the notice ready, Paul wrote notes for the hotel desk and for Jonny in the bar to say that he had a small accident. He would be back at work as soon as he was able.

Paul lay into the bed while Adrienne went out to deliver the messages.

He woke some time later with a start which brought severe pains to his ribs. He had been dreaming of a person drowning. It was as if he himself had been finding it difficult to draw his breath because he was under water. He wondered had it to do with Sandra and the big fellow or with that sailor whose bones he had probably played with many years before. Whatever had caused it he was glad to be awake and to be alive. "Maybe I am not as tough as I think," he thought, "or as cruel as Adrienne thinks."

Paul felt that Adrienne was right. He had become cruel. He was no longer the little boy who had freed the frogs Morgan had collected in a jamjar with holes in the lid. "None of God's creatures should be kept in captivity," he had said, a statement his mother had repeated with great gusto to her sisters or anyone else who would listen, to show what a kindhearted boy he was. "If she saw me yesterday," he thought, "she would not be going on about my sweet nature."

Later when Adrienne returned he asked her could he go with her to Ireland when she would be having the exhibition later in the year.

"I don't see why not," she said, "but will it be safe or sensible for you to appear there in public?"

"Nobody will recognise me after yesterday's facelift," he joked. "If I don't shave in the meantime I will have a bit of a disguise. Anyway it will be difficult to shave given the cuts on my face."

"You will be quite handsome with a beard."

Paul asked: "Are you saying that I am not handsome as I am?"

"You will be even more like Jesus with a beard."

"Don't be saying stuff like that."

"Why?" Adrienne asked. "Are you shy, or is it superstition?"

"A bit of both, maybe, but I don't want to draw any other trouble down on top of us."

"I was only joking," Adrienne said."

"Joke about something else.

"You are easily hurt," she said. "Those who say: "If you want to know me, come and live with me" are right."

"You think you have got to know me?" Paul asked.

"I'm getteing to know a little about you."

"What have you learnt?"

"That you are as sore as a brier today, in more senses than one, but you have every right to be after what happened yesterday. I don't know what you are like any other day."

"I was cruel yesterday, shy today, cranky now, not to speak of superstitious," Paul said: "What label have you ready for me tomorrow?"

"A big pet," Adrienne said, "if you carry on acting like a big child like you are at the moment."

Paul apologised. He blamed the previous day's beating and the stress he had been under all of that day when his life was in danger. I suppose there is such a thing as post-traumatic stress. If I was in the regular army I could be looking for compensation."

Adrienne went and gave him a hug as well as she could without hurting his wounds. "I have to admit to being a bit stressed myself these days," she said.

"Because of me?" Paul asked.

"Because of a lot more than that. Because my ex has just fathered a baby. Because I fear for both of us now that your cover has been blown. For the first time in my life I was looking behind me going down the street and getting on the vaperetto. Was I being followed? Even if I was, would I be smart enough to notice someone who was trained to do so."

Paul apologised again: "I'm getting out of here as fast as I can. It's not fair to you. I have brought all this stuff down on top of you."

"Don't go. Please," Adrienne said. "At this stage both of us are in it together. If you are being watched, I'm sure I have been seen as well."

Paul said he had made a decision about the uncertainty of his position: "I have decided to confront whatever is left of the movement when I go to Ireland. I'm going to find out is there a contract out on me or not."

"If they don't know where you are now, they will certainly know where you are then."

"I can't continue with the way thing are," Paul said. "It was alright when I was on my own, but if we are to be together . . ."

Adrienne answered that she would like that but she did not want either of them to be in trouble or in danger. Then, seemingly out of the blue, she said: "I want to have your baby."

"You mean now," he joked. "Can't you see the state that I am in."

"It could have happened already," Adrienne said.

"You are telling me you ae not on the pill or anything?"

"Don't worry. If it goes to that I will rear it myself, but I defintely want a baby. Your baby."

"Is this some kind of a rebound reaction because your former husband and his partner have had one?"

"I want to have a baby before I am too old," Adrienne said.

"You are still only a young one."

"The clock is tickng. I am in my mid thirties."

Paul was shaking his head: "This has come out of the blue. Would you not think that you should discuss this with a prospective father in advance? I am not sure that I am ready for this.""

Adrienne was blunt: "You don't lke children?"

"I haven't given the matter much thought. With the stuff I was involved in there was not much point in thinking about having children."

Adrienne rubbed her stomach with the palm of her hand: "It would hardly happen just like that. For all I know I may ever be able to have children. I was on the pill for so long because my husband didn't want them that my insides might be completely messed up."

The tension hung heavy in the apartment. Neither spoke for some time. Adrienne went out on the balcony and thought how much she would love a smoke. She seemed nervous and impatient when she returned but she did not say anything.

"What are we going to call him?" Paul asked after a while. "If it is a boy, that is."

"You mean to say that you are not completely against it?"

"You didn't answer my question," Paul said: "What name?"

"Giorgio," she answered.

"You know that Giorgio is not my real name."

"Who said I was thinking of you?" Adrienne asked. "I would call him after another great artist, Giorgio Armani. Not really. It would be after the handsome Italian boatman whose water-taxi I took in my first evening in Venice."

"Suppose it is a girl?"

Adienne said: "Venus."

"The goddess of love?"

"Guess again."

"Venus Williams, the great tenns player," Paul said.

"Third guess."

Paul shook his head: "I give up."

"Because it sounds like Venice, the loveliest city in the world, the place the two of us met."

"Where do I stand in all this?" Paul asked some time later. "Am I just the stallion that provides the sperm?"

"Not a bad stallion either, if I remember correctly."

"I'm serious," Paul said.

"Is it not a man's greatest fantasy? A stallion without responsibility. A stallion without conscience. I would not ask for any support if you wanted to have nothing to do with it."

"What you are saying is that you don't care if we are together or not, so long as you can have a baby?"

Adrienne explained: "I'd love us to be together and to have a family, but I don't want to tie you down if you want to be free."

"Do you think I would have no interest in my own child even if I was tricked into having it?"

"I would hope that you would," Adrienne said, "but that would be up to you. I could manage on my own."

"I would not be happy with that kind of an arrangement."

Adrienne could not hide her sarcasm: "You could always shoot me, or take me out to sea and let me drown."

"That is a good enoug reason not to have a child with you," he said. "You would be throwing things like that at me for the rest of my life, and saying it front of the children as well when you would be angry."

Adrienne grabbed her handbag and headed for the door. When Paul asked where she was going she said it was probably not too late to get the morning after pill: "It should work after two days."

"Stop," Paul said. "There is too much happening too quickly. I didn't expect such intense discussion on a hypothetical matter, on a maybe. I thought I had enough trouble yesterday."

"So now I am trouble?"

Paul stretched out a hand: "Come here to me. What are we really arguing about?"

"About a child that we don't have and probably won't have."

They kissed and the tension faded.

Some time later Adrienne asked Paul about the women who had been in his life. He dodged the question as best he could: "You are not the first woman I have been with, and from what you have told me I am not the first man to be with you. So we are even."

"You will not get away with that," Adrienne said. "I was only with one man, and there is not much to tell about that except that we eventually separated, because he was unfaithful. Now what about your women of all nationalities?"

"I did not ask you to tell me anything. You volunteered. I know from experience that talk like that just leads to jealousy."

"So I have reason to be jealous?" Adrienne asked: "Is there a wife and children stashed away some place?"

"That is exactly my point," Paul commented. "You will pick something from everything I say. You should have been a barrister." He did admit some time later that most of the women he had slept with were with him for no more than one or two nights.

"Was that because of your work?"

"That, and the fact that I never met anyone like you," Paul said.

"I'm sure you told the very same thing to every one of your one-night stands. To get them into bed with you"

"You are different," Paul said with all sincerity: "Any other woman would have run a mile if she heard all that you have about my life in the past week or so. You are still with me."

"Is it because you have not really lived with a woman that you were so contrary with me all morning?" Adrienne asked.

"What is your excuse? There could be some truth in it. I was used to other people around me in college, or while in training camps. Nobody ever accused me of being cranky."

Adrienne pointed towards the sunshine coming from the window of the balcony: "Why don't we forget ourselves for a while and enjoy the beauty of the evening and of the city?"

"There is nothing wrong with that," Paul joked, "if you can keep your mouth shut for a few seconds at a time."

Despite his injuries and the stiffness of his body from the previous day's ordeal, Paul struggled out onto the balcony: "There is something I would like to do out here," he said, "when my wounds are healed."

"And have all of Venice watching? That would be fun alright. For all the viewers."

"Nobody would see anything at nightime."

Adrienne stood by his side and breathed in the sea air. Polluted or not, it made her feel better: "That is what I do when I am dying for a fag," she said. "It eases the craving."

Paul tried to follow her example, but only succeeded in hurting his sides: "I hope the smoke of the city is no worse than that of the cigarettes. When you think of all the emissions from the exhausts and chimneys of all the boats," he said, "not to speak of the raw sewerage."

"I'm sure the sea and the tides wash away the worst of it," Adrienne said.

Paul had more knowledge of the sea: "If the water was deep enough, or if the tide rose and fell as much as it does around our coasts at home, it might flush out all the dirt. Tides around here barely rise or fall."

They went inside then, because there was a cool breeze outside on the balcony, despite the sunshine. When Patrick called later, Adrienne told him that she was busy, that she had no time to talk to him. He was not listening and blurted out that Sheila was only going to allow him see their child for a couple of hours every week.

"Are you crying?" Adrienne asked.

She knew he was covering up for what he would have considered a weakness when he said he had a headcold. It's not that I am worried about, but the attitude of this bitch who brought my child into the world."

Adrienne asked: "How often do you want to see him each week?"

"Anytime I want to," Patrick told her. "There was no talk about this until the child was born. I'd say it is the father and mother that are putting her up to it. So that I would pay more maintainence. They are making a bargaining tool of the poor baby."

"You will hardly want to see him every day," Adrienne reasoned. "Won't you be working all week as usual?"

"I will, but that is not the point."

"Would you be happy to see him maybe two days a week?" Adrienne asked him. "That would appear to be reasonable enough. A bit more when he is bigger and you can take him to the park or to a football match."

Patrick wanted to dig in his heels: "That is all well and good, but it is the principle that is is important. Is this the first step in not allowing me to see him at all?"

"Fuck the principle," was Adrienne's attitude. "Get your foot in the door, and take what you are getting just now. When you have proven yourself a good Dad you can ask for more."

"Why do I need to prove anything?" Patrick asked. "There is no question about paternity. I have rights or I haven't. So far I have just been told what I can or can not do."

"Maybe she hopes that you will marry her," Adrienne suggested. "Then you could see the boy every day."

"Hoping she will be," Patrick said. "She has got more cranky and contrary every day since the child was born."

"She probably isn't getting much sleep."

"Whose side are you on?" Patrick asked Adrienne.

"I'm no expert but I have met enough mothers to know that hormones play away with them after giving birth. Then there is the whole question of post natal depression."

"Do you mean that she is gone off her rocker?" Patrick asked. "Could she harm the child?"

"I'm sure she is fine. I'm just telling you that it is often a difficult time for a woman. Her emotions can be all over the place. I would cut her a bit of slack if I were you, and things will probably work out alright."

Patrick was obviously not listening to her: "I'm not putting up with it," he said. "I am the father and I have rights."

"Of course you have," Adrienne assured him. "If things do not improve you could see a solicitor."

"I thought of that," he said, "but that might drive her over the edge altogether, and she would not let me see him at all."

"You could discuss the implications with your solcitor, Patrick. I don't have the answers."

"I was not expecting an answer, but I needed to talk to someone," Patrick said Adrienne was tempted to say: "A pity you didn't consider all of this before you loosened the belt of your trousers, but she had said that often enough. This was not the time or the place. She felt a sense of shame that deep down she had a feeling of satisfaction that things were not working out for himself and Sheila. A couple of months earlier she would have been pleased to have a kind of revenge on those two who had blighted her life, but she had moved on to some extent. It was pity she had for them now more than anything.

"We will talk more about this again, Patrick," Adrienne said. "I have company at the moment."

"Is that fellow still with you?"

"We are all grown-ups now, I hope."

"I have one more question," Patrick said. He sounded as if he was trying to hold on a little longer to what had once been an anchor in his life: "Has a father any say in what name his child is called?"

"That is another question for your solicitor," Adrienne answered. "As far as I know that depends on whether the couple is married or agree on a name. Do you not like what she wants to call him?"

"She is talking of calling him Emmanuel. Isn't there a dirty pcture with that name?"

"I have heard talk of it, but it is the female version of the name in so far as I know—Emanuelle. I always thought it a nice name for a man. I don't remember much of my Christian doctrine, but Emannuel was a name given to Jesus. It meant something like 'God is with us' So you might have found Jesus after all."

"It's not Jesus she is thinking about but some soccer player in England." Patrick said.

Adrienne tried to give her former husband some advice: "When you are talking about the mother of your child, you should call her by her name, Sheila. Give her that much dignity, or you will be at loggerheads all your lives."

"I don't know do I want to have anything to do with her," Patrick answered in a depressed tone.

"There must have been something between you last year," Adrienne reminded him.

Patrick let a big sigh: "That was then and this is now. It was the biggest mstake in my life."

"If you want to have a relationship with your son . . ." Adrienne felt there was no need to say any more."

"You are as bossy now as you ever were," Patrick said. "Don't tell me what I should or shouldn't do."

Adrienne felt herself get angry: "I was just trying to give you a bit of advice. I've given it now. You know I have a visitor, but you kept talking. I have a life too."

Patrick sounded more contrite: "I thought the visitor thing was just to put me off, because you didn't want to talk to me."

"Well, you were wrong about that and you were wrong about what you said to me the last time we talked."

"What was that?"

Adrienne looked around to see was Paul in earshot before answering: "You said that you were the only man I would ever be with. Well that is not true any more."

Patrick did not answer. He had hung up the phone.

Paul came back into the living room: "Who is the cruel one now?"

"You shouldn't have been listening to a private conversation."

"What chance did I have when you had the loudspeaker on? There is nowhere else to go in this apartment."

"I tend to forget that I am not here on my own." Adrienne sat down as if the wind had been knocked from her sails. "As for being cruel, I actually tried to be kind and understanding, but he still managed to rile me at the end of it all. We have learned nothing about communication in our ten years together."

Paul was curious: "Is it really true that the only man you were with before me was your husband?"

"None of your business," Adrienne answered stiffly. "You should not have been listening. Anyway I may have been telling a pack of lies."

"It didn't sound like that to me. Isn't it nice when you think about it. Almost a virgin."

"I will revert to being one if you don't shut up about it," she said.

Paul continued to probe: "Even when you were a teenager. Did you not ever try it? Out of curiousity."

"Not everybody is a slut," Adrienne said sharply.

"That is the last word I would apply to you."

"I'm thinking more of Sheila, the woman who stole my husband."

"You need two to tango," Paul commented.

"He is paying dearly for it now, and I have no sympathy for him. I have even less sympathy for the one that bore his child."

Paul was amused by one remark of Patrick's: "That was funny about the child's name, Emannuel.

That took him over the border of propriety in so far as Adrienne was concerned. She defended her former husband: "He may not be as up to date as others on what is going on in the world. Not everyone belongs to the whizz-kid communication revolution."

"Are you starting to feel that this place is too small for the both of us?" Paul asked.

"I am just not used to it, to being together all the time. The apartment is too small. I don't have room to think my own thoughts. I need a bit of time to work things out in my head."

xxii

ADRIENNE TRAVELLED BY VAPERETTO TOWARDS the centre of the city the following morning. The way in which the large boat glided along the surface of the water gave her a kind of peace. Because she had an open ticket and was in no hurry she stayed on board all the way to the end of its course. She took the next one back to where she wanted to go. The first boat had been fairly full with people who seemed to be on their way to work. The tourists for the most part had not stirred out yet from their hotels or apartments, not to speak of the great liners that came to the mouth of the harbour.

She surveyed the buildings on one side of the canal while going in one direction, the ones on the other side coming back. While she was looking at them she was observing little more than their outline. What she was soaking in was the sturdy contentment provided by this workboat as it chugged along, solid and workmanlike as it went about its business.

Adrienne banished the questions that had preyed on her mind to rest in so far as she could as they sailed along. She left the boat close to Ponte del Sospiri, by the Bridge of Sighs. She thought that name suited the mood of the past few days. Her heart lifted as she stood on top of the bridge, high above the water watching the various sizes and shapes of boat ply their various trades beneath. She emitted a couple of deep sighs of her own, and that seemed to help ease her mind and feelings a little. There were crowds of people all around, people selling pictures and masks, handbags with false celebrity labels, beggars as always, while others just hurried by as they went about their business.

Adrienne was pleased to think that she would soon be back in Ireland, and better again, on the Atlantic shore with the southwest wind blowing through her hair. She went through the things she needed to prepare in advance, especially now that Paul would probably travel with her. She would leave it to the gallery to arrange everything that had to do with the pictures. She knew now that Venice, as attractive and all as it was, would never really become home. It would be fine for a time, though, until Patrick and her marriage and all the baggage involved had been put behind her,

Adrienne imagined herself at her house in Wcklow painting away contentedly. Her little girl, Venus would be running about or messing with her paints. She might also do as her mother before had done, help her father to plant potatoes and vegetables. She remembered how she had once pulled up the carrots and left the weeds. Her excuse was that they could plant the carrots on a ridge that had no weeds. It had set tham back a little but her strategy had eventually worked.

With all that had happened in recent days, Adrienne realised that she had overlooked her father, despite her promise to ring him more often. She tried his number on her mobile phone but there was no reply. She left a message to say that she was thinking of him on The Bridge of Sighs. She said she would be back in Ireland quite soon for her exhibition and would see him then

"Where is he?" She wondered was there something wrong with her father when he did not answer his phone. She imagined him lying in a pool of blood on the floor of the bathroom after getting a stroke, with nobody there to look after him. What about the woman who went in to do the cleaning? What about the woman he went for walks with? "He has a better social life than I have," she told herself. She made a resolution that she would not allow herself worry unnecessarily about him.

Adrienne wondered should she invite the woman who went walking in the mountains with her father to the exhibition. It made her feel disloyal to her mother in some way. She reminded herself that this was a time to look forward, to be positive. Her mother was gone but her father was alive, and she could not expect him to spend the rest of his life mourning her mother. He was getting on with his life, but she was not. Well, not really. She needed to put the life that was past behind her, but there Patrick was, night after night like a ghost hovering over the smithereens of their marriage. It was time for her to tell him to stop ringing, to get on with his own life. Had she the heart to do it when he was feeling so low?

Feeling hungry, Adrienne came down from the bridge and made her way to a small trattoria from which she would have a view of the canal. She ordered vegetable soup, a slice of pizza and a glass of white wine. Sitting there enjoying the view she wondered was Patrick expecting to be invited to her exhibition. Perhaps she should ask Sheila to come with him. It might help them to come to an arrangement about the child if they were treated as a couple. She reminded herself that this was none of her business. Whatever trouble they were in was of their own making. She decided not to invite either of them. This would show that she had moved on.

Although the sun was in her eyes and there was a glare on the water, Adrienne was sure that she could see Paul's water-taxi at the other side of the canal heading towards the area his apartment was in. He seemed to be wearing the type of hat and striped jersey worn by gondoliers. "He has made a right scarecrow of himself now," she thought, in what must be an effort to disguise himself.

Feeling that he must have remarkable powers of recovery or that he was involved in some dodgy activity she decided to return to her apartment sooner than she had intended to check if has there. Whatever he was involved in should have nothing to do with her, but at the same time she did not want him to get into any more trouble. Having been targeted by a drugs gang earlier in the week, she began to wonder could he possibly be involved in drug running himself.

Just then Adrienne noticed a welldressed handsome man sitting a few tables away who seemed to be watching her. One or other of them dropped their eyes every time they looked straight at each other. She began to feel a cold sweat break out on her back, despite the sunshine. Thinking there was only one way to find out had he anything to do with Paul or those who searched for him, she went over boldly and asked why was he staring at her. He opened his hands with a big dramatic gesture and asked in English that was heavily accented was it a crime now to look at a beautiful woman. Adrienne found herself laughing out loud in a mixture of relief and embarrassment. She thanked him for the compliment and gracefully left the premesis.

xxiii

Paul took his opportunity to catch up on lost sleep as soon as Adrienne left the apartment that morning. He had not taken pain-killers the night before because of the nightmares they had given him previously. That had left his two sides and his face painful. Every time he was close to sleep Adrienne stirred in the bed and accidentally touched one of his wounds. He did not have the heart to wake her so he just lay there feeling sorry for himself. Feeling that he was less likely to have bad dreams in the light of day he had dosed himself heavily in the morning and fallen into a deep and drugged sleep.

It was not a dream that awoke him but the need to vomit. He had no idea where the grey bile that surfaced from his stomach came from but he had rarely felt so bad in his life. It left a terrible taste in his mouth. He washed his teeth and rinsed his mouth with everything he could find to get rid of the bad taste, but nothing seemd to work. Before he knew it he was asleep again and did not wake for a few hours.

Paul felt somewhat better when he awoke, but he knew that he needed to get out of that apartment and back to his own as soon as possible. He considered that Adrienne might have been right when she said that he had no experience of living with a womwn. This was the time that he usually parted with women who had stayed over, the time at which pleasure and passion was not enough to sustain some kind of a relationship. One of his mates had been known to say: "Talking time is getting out of there time." Not all of their altercations had been his fault. Adrienne tended to fly off the handle quickly too. He felt it was time for him to settle down and have children, but perhaps he was not made for that kind of life. Some people were drifters who were not able to settle down. Maybe he was one of those.

An uncle of Paul's on his mother's side had left home at the age of fifteen, and nothing had been heard of him until he died in a Glasgow bedsitter sixty years later. He had been away but had obviously never forgotten his roots. Local newspapers from the west of Ireland had been found under his bed, items to do with his home place underlined in red ink. There had never been a night during his own youth that his mother had not said a prayer for her brother who had, to all extents and purposes, disappeared. She was probably praying for himself now in the same way. He was her dead son as far as she was concerned, but he was probably more like his uncle, a wanderer. The body was brought home from Scotland for burial. Paul had never seen the man alive, but there was something about him that appealed to him as he lay, cold and dignified in his coffin at the wake.

Paul thought that if he and Adrienne were to continue their relationship, the best plan might be to maintain separate apartments and see each other from time to time. They would not be under each other's feet in that way. The reason he was in her apartment at the moment was because he was hurt, not because they had decided to live together. That had contributed to the tension between them. They needed time for a bit of courtship before moving in together. They might eventually settle down together, but they really needed to get to know each other first.

"You just want to escape commitment," Paul told himself. Would he be eying up other women if he was back in his aparthment on his own? Eyeing maybe, but that was all. It was all or nothing if they were to continue together. The little break they were having that day would probably help. The longer term prospects of having to live in the shadows of his past hung over them at all times. They could not spend their lives on the lookout for special branch detectives, former members of the movement, drug dealers on the lookout for revenge. He would need to settle those matters once and for all.

An idea that had occurred to him before and which he had dismissed from his mind was becoming more attractive. What if he was to come out of the closet, come back from the living dead? What if he was to sell his story to a newspaper, the story of his life, the story of his faked death, the story of his rising from the dead as a Venice water-taxi driver. That would certainly be interesting, and he could probably get the price of a house or apartment from the telling. Would that keep the wolves from the door? Would former comrades still be trying to kill him, or would they fear for their part in the democratic process if they or anyone belonging to them had him taken out? As for the druggies, they would leave themselves much more open to suspicion if he was killed. The other scenario was that they would hire a proper assassin rather than the bungling fools that had come to kill him earlier that week

It might be stupid to blow his cover, Paul thought. It seemed to have been by accident that Sandra and her mate had discovered him, but how many others had they told? If his secret came out where could he go? Would Adrienne join him in some other city or country? She had her own life and her art. She could never have another exhibition without coming out in the open. She was cranky enough already without asking her to give up the painting. There was some cover at present in that nobody knew of their relationship. That would end if they went to the Irish exhibition together. The last thing he wanted was to put her in any danger.

There was still something attractive about the other plan. Paul imagined the headline: "The Spy Who Came Back From The Dead." It was one possible way out, but there were implications. Would the Democratic Unionist Party pull out of government with Sinn Féin because they had not been told the full truth? That some of the dead were still alive and well and living overseas. He had once been "Public Enemy Number One" in the tabloid newspapers. His faked death had brought the comment: "May he rot in hell" from one Unionist politician. He could hardly expect any sympaty if he returned unrotten from the dead.

The positive side of it all, Paul thought, was that he was still alive and well, and in love. He was looking forward to Adrienne coming back so that he could consult her about his plan to come clean and face the consequenses. She might have different ideas, but they would consider all their options carefully.

xxiv

"WHERE DID YOU GO IN the boat?" Adrienne was barely inside the door of the apartment when she asked that question.

Paul woke up suddenly and put his head above the blanket which covered him on the chaise longue: "Has the boat been stolen?" was his first reaction. He struggled towards the balcony and looked down to where his taxi was tied: "She is there where I left her," he said as he came back into the living room.

"I could tell you myself that it is there," Adrienne said, "but I thought I saw you on the canal a while ago."

Paul replied: "I never left this room. I lay down on that thing and had one of the best sleeps I had for a long time."

"I could have sworn I saw you in the boat with a striped jersey and a gondoliers' hat when I sat having something to eat."

"There must have been something in your coffee. It sounds like a dream to me."

Adrienne shook her head: "I must be losing it."

"A lot of boats look alike," Paul said. "Were you hoping I had taken off out of your life?"

"Something like that," Adrienne said lightly. "What really surprised me was that you were fit enough to drive it."

"I'm not even able to make a cup of coffee, never mind going down those stairs."

"Is that a hint? Do you want your slavegirl to get you a cup?"

"I'll get it myself after a while. What I really need is some help in getting dressed. I can hardly raise my right arm. He threw aside the blanket that covered part of his body and proceeded to remove his shorts with his left hand."

"Do you have to do that in the living room?" Adrienne asked.

"There is more space than in the bathroom. Anyway I thought you had seen me naked before now."

"Suppose someone walks in?"

"Are you expecting someone?" Paul asked.

"I just said supposing they do."

"I'm sorry," Paul tried to cover himself. "I thought an artist would be more open. The world of bohemia and all that."

"I suppose the next thing you will do is atand out bollock-naked on the balcony."

"I hadn't thought of that," he said. "What is this really all about? I don't think it is about a lack of clothes. Do you want me to leave the apartment or what?"

"I don't think that your health is good enough yet."

"But you would like me to go when it is?" Paul asked.

"That depends on how we are getting on in the meantime."

"I could go home and sleep in my own apartment," Paul said, "but I would need some help with meals and that kind of thing. At least I would not be under your feet all of the time."

Adrienne did not rule out that possibility: "Would you be safe in that apartment, after what happened last week?"

Paul answered with another question: "Is anywhere really safe?" He explained that he was thinkng of contacting a journalist in order to tell his story and see what would happen as a result of that.

"If you are telling your story, leave me out of it," Adrienne said. "I can see the headlines already: 'Artist harbours sniper.' Or 'The abstract artist and the living dead man.'"

"I'm just considering the idea," Paul explained: "I would have no notion of dragging you into it."

"But you would be there at my exhibition. How would I explain who you are? My bodyguard?"

"If I was telling my story in that way I would stay out of the limelight. For a while anyway. Like everything else it would be a nine-day wonder and the tabloid sharks would move on to someone or something else."

Adrienne told him she thought his previous plan was better: "Speak to the leaders of the movement. If that does not work, turn to plan B—publicity."

"You could have a good point there," Paul said. "It would give me leverage with the leaders if they thought there was a danger of the story coming out. They would have to deal with the kind of a limbo in which the likes of me has been left."

Adrienne had another idea: "Why don't you write your own story, and not bother with journalists?"

"I'm no writer. It's about as much as I can do to write my own name."

"I could help you," Adrienne said. "My lap-top is there. We might get on better if both of us had something to do."

"I can only really use one hand at the moment."

"Can't you hammer away with one finger?" Adrienne said.

"I have a laptop in my apartment for my accounts and for keeping in touch with what is happening back home, but I have never done anything but figures on it. I have never written anything."

"One finger might be enough to start with, until you get the hang of it," Adrienne said.

"It would probably keep us from fighting and arguing anyway."

"I doubt it. Reasonably strong characters tend to bounce off each other in that way."

Paul repeated: "reasonably strong characters," after her. "You are unbeatable in an argument. Extremely strong character I would say."

Adrienne laughed: "I will let you win an argument soon." She went over to her lap-top and turned it on, opened a blank page and stood back: "Start anytime you want. Ask for help if you need it."

"Paul seemed to be taken aback: "Do you mean to start now? Immediately?"

"There is no time like the present. The most useful button of the whole lot is the delete one. If you make a mistake or make a mess of half of it, you can get rid of it in a second and start again."

Paul did his beat to postpone the project: "I would prefer to write on the lap-top that I have in my own apartment."

"You can start on this one," Adrienne explained, "and just transfer it from one to the other by e-mail. You can use this as a word processor when you are here and the other one in your own place."

Paul shook his head: "It looks like there is going to be no escape."

"Have a go at it, and see what happens," Adrienne tried to encourage him. He sat down and tapped a few letters awkwardly."

"Will you be reading what I write?" Paul asked.

"Not when you are not here. I will read it with you if you want me to help you."

"I can't bear to do anything with someone looking over my shoulder," Paul said.

"I can understand that perfectly, as I am like that when I am painting. I will only come and read something if you ask me to."

Paul made another attempt to try and avoid writing: "English is not my first language. There will be neither head or tail to it."

"Write it in Irish so," Adrienne suggested. "It will put the whole country reading Gaelic to find out what you have to say."

"I would be delighted to see that day, but unfortunately I won't."

"That was the ambition of the painter and novelist, George Moore," Adrienne explained: "When he returned to Dublin from France more than a hundred years ago he said he was going to write a book in Gaelic that would be so good the whole of the country would want to read it."

"He didn't manage it?" Paul asked.

"Unfortunately no."

"Did he even have Irish?"

"Apparently he had learnt some from the servant girls in Moore Hall, the family home in Mayo. That book that will put half of Ireland reading Gaelic has still to be written. Why don't you write it?"

"I'm afraid to even try," Paul said.

"Why? What are you afraid of?" Adrienne asked.

"I am not a writer or a book man."

"Have a go and see where it gets you."

"I'll start when I get back to my full health."

Adrienne put on the pressure: "Write one word, one line."

"I don't know where or how to even start," Paul answered.

"Start at the beginning," was Adrienne's answer to that. "like James Joyce and the moocow going down the road."

"That is silly, childish stuff," Paul said.

"It was good enough for James Joyce. It was just his way of starting at the beginning."

"Where am I supposed to start?" Paul asked. "At he beginning of the Troubles in Northern Ireland or at the beginning of my life?"

"I would suggest your life," Adrienne said.

"Who would be interested in that?"

"It would show where you came from, what prompted you to go in the direction you did."

"I was a bit of an idealist, I suppose."

"Ho did that come about?" Adrienne asked.

"From reading mainly."

"There you are," she said.

"There you are what?"

"Your story, what led you to where you are now."

"A long story," Paul said.

"Exactly, and that is what people will want to read, to hear."

"I still don't know where to start."

Adrienne asked: "What is your earliest memory?"

"I can see my grandmother in my mind's eye, She is coming down a path to the house with newlylaid eggs she has just gathered from the hens in her apron. That was when she got the stroke and all the eggs broke on the ground."

"What an image for the collapse of the Northern State after the Civil Right's movement began," Adrienne said.

"But it had nothing to do with that."

"It is your earliest memory, the beginning of your story, the story of how you got to be here battered and bruised today. Write it down."

"I don't see how it has anything to do with anything." Paul said.

"Write it down," Adrienne ordered. "You can always delete it again if you don't want to use it. That is the beauty of the word processor."

"I would prefer to write about how I got involved in the Troubles," Paul said. "About the hunger strikes and all of that."

"Ok, write what comes easiest first. Again at this stage you don't need a beginning, a middle and an end. You can write down everything that comes to you and rearrange it all by cutting and pasting later.

Paul was still not convinced: "I think t would be better to get a journalist, someone who knows the job."

"Someone with his own prejudices and point of view. Do you want it to be your story or his?"

"Mine of course. Ok, I'll have a go. As you say I can always delete half or all of it."

Paul began very slowly, thinking for a while and then painstakingly tapping out what he decided to write with one finger. He slowly got into a rhythm as he thought of what he considered to be small but significant happenings from his youth. Adrienne sketched him as he concentrated on what he wanted to write. She considered that was the kind of life she would like them to have together as a couple, each working away and concentrating on what they had to do without bothering the other. They would get together for a meal and a chat at the end of the day. Neither spoke for a long time, until Paul had completed a page.

"I could get a feel for this," Paul said. "It is not as difficult as I had anticipated. The grammar and spelling are a bit of a mess, but one story grows into another after a while."

"Don't worry too much about spelling or that kind of stuff," Adrienne assured him. "That is what editors are for. If you have a story to tell, there are experts in those areas to correct it."

"Would you like to read what I have written?" Paul asked.

"I would love to." Adrienne read through it and complimented him, while adding: "I feel that you leapt too far ahead from when you were a child. You seem to have grown up in the first page."

"You told me to write what came into my head."

"What do you remember about when you were at primary school?"

"I read a lot," he said, We didn't have a television at that stage."

Adrienne tried to draw him out: "Was it comics or books or newspapers?"

"Everything from cowboy stories by Zane Gray to Dan Breen's "My Fight For Irish Freedom." I thought Dan was a bit of a cowboy himself, but I loved him." He told of the time he had mentioned to his parents that it was a pity there were no more Black and Tans to kill."

"Write that down," Adrienne told him, "and everything like it you can think of. It will show people why you choose to go down the road of life that you did."

"That was not the first road that I chose." He told of the idealism and naievity perhaps that had led him to go to Rome to study for the priesthood.

"What led you to do that?"

Paul was getting exasperated: "Amn't I after telling you."

"I know already. It is not me you have to convince but your readers." Adrienne told him that asking homself: "Why did I do this or that?" was a good way of establishing his motives before writing them down.

They took a break for coffee. Standing out on the balcony they continued their discussion. Paul returned to the word processor while Adrienne cooked fresh fish and pasta and arranged a generous salad for their evening meal. By the time it was ready she was finding it hard to get Paul to the dinner table.

"If you write too much at once," she said, "you will get fed up of it, and eventually you will not want to go back to it."

He joined her as soon as he had finished his train of thought: "My mother always said that I was like a dog with a bone. When I take an interest in something I give it my full attention. I know that it is like a disease, but that is how I have always worked, whether it was doing something like I am doing now, or working at home at hay or turf."

"What have I let myself in for?" Adrienne said. "Living with a writaholic."

"That is how it will probably be until I am fit enough to go back to work in the water-taxi," Paul answered. "Is it not better than to be moping around and getting in the way of your painting?"

"Don't go too crazy on me," Adrienne said.

Paul was already planning ahead: "If I bring my own lap-top with me when I go back to work, I will be able to get a few pages written while waiting for passengers at the airport."

Adrienne teased: "Better still, you will be able to write as you drive along. You can get one of the tourists to steer for you."

"I will have to start looking for a publisher," Paul suggested.

"One thing at a time. You will need to have a lot of words on screen before you interest a publisher."

Paul was getting carried away: "Even if they kill me when I have part of it written, there will be enough of a story out there to tell what things were like for people like me who were sidelined by the movement."

Adrienne tried to rein in his enthusiasm: "One thing at a time. Don't get too far ahead of yourself. Writing is slow hard difficult work. I have friends who write, and I would much prefer to be painting pictures."

"It's fine for you," Paul said. "You have talent. Talent and reputation. There will always be buyers for what you paint."

"It's a bit like what they say about sportspeople. You are as good as your last ace or your last match. I am as good as my last painting. Even then it might not attract a buyer."

"I wish I could understand the abstract stuff," Paul commented.

"I can't say I always understand it myself," was Adrienne's take on it, "but it works for me."

Paul was getting lost in his own ambition: "How many words does it take to write a normal full-length book?"

"Sixty to eighty thousand words would be a good start in so far as I know," Adrienne told him. "A few thousand more could be added during rewriting and editing. An awful lot of words."

"How many do you think I have done this evening?"

"Five hundred, six hundred," she said.

Paul calculated: "Twice that in a day. Sixty days. I could have it done in two months."

"Better you than me," Adrienne said. "Good luck to you. I hope you avoid writer's block and lazy days. No hangovers. If you can manage that I will definitely have a writaholic on my hands."

Paul planned out loud: "I will not go back on the boat until I am finished. I will do like Dan Breen and Tom Barry and Ernie O'Malley in days gone by. I will write my own story and it will be as good as any of them."

"You are frightening me," Adrienne said.

"Frigtening you? How?"

"You are like one of those people who joins a new religion or political movement. What do they call it? The zeal of the converted. It is the worst disease of all as far as I am concerned."

"Isn't it good that I didn't take to the drink with the same zeal," Paul suggested.

"I don't know what to make of you," Adrienne said with a smile.

"I'm just mad crazy. Apart from that I am a nice enough kind of a bloke."

Adrienne told him of some of her doubts about him: "I thought you were involved in some kind of a scam earlier when I was sure it was your boat I saw out on the water."

"What did you yink that I was up to?"

"I did think of drugs, seeing that was part of a drug mob that was after you the last day. I saw your boat outside when I returnrd, but I still was not sure had you been there and back. I just don't know what to think half of the the time."

Paul asked: "What you are really saying is that you don't trust me?"

"I want to. I want to believe you. I want to trust you. I know now that you were not capable of moving the boat today because of your arm, but I feel that I still don't know you."

"I don't know what to do to convince you that I am genuine," Paul said. "Time is the only thing that will tell that. Is there anything else that you need to tell me while you are at it?"

Having your boat tied outside at the steps is like having a sign up that you are staying here. I think that it puts us both in danger."

"I don't think that I am capable of moving it. I'll ask one of the other lads to do it for me."

"Could I be an extra pair of hands for you?" Adrienne asked. "If you can drive it, I can loosen and tie the ropes again."

"Let's do it now then and it will ease your mind."

As they were getting ready to leave the apartment Paul drew attention to a news item on the radio which was switched on in the background. The body of a man had been picked up in a fishing net in the Adriatic. He was wearing a life-jacket and may have fallen from a passing ship. The Coastguard were investigating what looked like bloodstains on his hands.

"My blood," Paul said. "He punched me often enough."

"Would the seawater not have washed it off?" Adrienne asked.

"It was well dried on by the time we left the apartment."

"What are you going to do?"

"Nothing," Paul answered. "It would be a very long shot to make a connection with me. He was obviously a long way offshore."

"Any mention of the girl?" Adrienne explained that she did not grasp what had been spoken so quickly in Italian."

"No mention," Paul said. "When they identify him or both of them for that matter, I don't think the authorities will shed a lot of tears. It will be a case of 'good riddance.'"

"Is there blood in the boat?" Adrienne asked, "and in the apartment?"

Paul explained: "I cleaned the boat as best I could with saltwater on the way back. I must have been running on adrenalin at that stage. The apartment is another matter."

"Can you get someone to clean it?"

"I would be as well to put up my hands and say that I am guilty if the forensic crowd examine the apartment," Paul said. "I'll have to clean it myself as best I can."

"I'll help you," Adrienne promised.

"I don't want to get you involved.

"I am already involved. Up to my neck. Anyway you can't do it without help." Adrienne helped Paul to limp as far as the boat. She freed the ropes. The engine jumped smoothly into life in spite of not having been used for a couple of days. Paul steered it with one hand as they moved slowly out into the canal. As they met each vaperetto he moved the water-taxi further out into the middle and then across near the other side to its usual berth. Adrienne followed Paul's instructions, tying up with ropes and a chain which was padlocked. The tarpaulin was then tied on with short pieces of twine.

"I won't touch er for a month," Paul said, "until the pains are gone and that story nearly written."

"You would think you were talking about a woman," Adrienne said, "the way you always call it she or her."

"Boats were always feminine," Paul answered "Like horses. In Conamara. Even a stallion is referred to as she."

"A stallion with a feminine side," Adrienne mused. "Now that would be interesting."

She did most of the cleaning in the apartment, although Paul tried to steer a mop around the floor with one hand. Adrienne was pessimistic: "All the cleaning in the world will not prevent forensic experts from finding traces of something."

"You have been watching too many crime scene investigations on telly," was Paul's answer to that. "Any blood they find will be mine. Who knows who stayed in the apartment before me if they find anything else? Anyway I can't see them making a connection."

"Should you show your face in the Principe?" Adrienne asked when the clean-up was finished.

"I don't want anyone to see me with my face black and blue and yellow. They would think that I was wearing one of those fancy masks."

Paul sat down in front of the word processor as soon as they got back to Adrienne's apartment. He started to type again with one finger as he had done earlier.

"Adrienne did not seem to be very satisfied: "I thought we were going to relax for a while and go to bed early."

"Sure we never stopped talking all evening," was Paul's answer to that. "Why don't you do your own thing. Have a shower or a bath or something. I will be after you in a little while."

"I wish that you were after me now," was Adrienne's throwaway phrase as she left the room. Paul did not hear, or just ignored it: "My head is full of stuff that I have to write down. If I don't it will all be gone clear out of my mind."

Adrienne returned some time later from her bath in a loose silk dressing gown, with a perfume that filled the room with a beautiful scent. She pointed at the laptop: "So you prefer that rectangular face to mine?" she asked.

Paul kept writing: "You know that I prefer nothing or nobody to you."

"Prove it so." Adrienne began to massage his shoulders.

"You are hurting me," he groaned. "You know that I am not fit for that stuff. I just want to finish writing down what is in my mind."

"That means more to you than us?" Adrienne asked.

Paul answered with his own question: "What would you do if you had a picture in your imagination that you wanted to get down on canvas? Would you not blot out everything else until you had it painted?"

"I would put a person before a painting or a story," she answered.

"Alright so." Paul began to reluctantly save and close down the computer.

"Don't bother," Adrienne said. "I know where I stand."

XXV

THERE WERE SO MANY THOUGHTS and memories flooding through Paul's mind that it reminded him of the stream close to his parent'sl home after a rainstorm. It went from being a trickle to a torrent in a matter of minutes, sweeping all before it on its desperate hurry to the shore. The worst thing about his torrent of memory was that it was completely disorganised. Memories of his youth mixed up with those that had to do with lining up a sniping target in his rifle sights. These mixed with happy times he shared with colleagues in Rome while a student.

What he really wanted to write about at this stage was when he was a young boy growing up, but that was being crowded by images from later in life. He wrote down the thoughts that interfered with those to do with his youth on scraps of paper which were scattered all around him. He was aware of Adrienne's anger with him but he put that to the back of his mind as he imagined it. He would deal with that later. Despite his injuries he felt she would turn to him as he got into bed and welcome him with open arms, all forgiven, pain extinguished by big generous kisses before being welcomed into her inner sanctum.

In the meantime there was work to be done. Paul read through what he had written already. He edited it as best he could, busy with the delete button before tapping in replacement words and sentences. His mind wandered then to black and white pictures on their first television, a civil rights march in Northern Ireland, shouts of "One man, one vote," policemen charging and battering the marchers, black blood on white faces. The name of the place, Burntollet had been etched forever on his mind.

Atrocities on both sides had led young men and women of both religious persuasions, Protestant and Roman Catholic to take up the cudgels on behalf of what they considered to be their people. These 'cudgels' took the shape of bombs and bullets, or in his own case the long, clean, well-oiled rifle. He had always consoled himself with the fact that most of what he had done had been clean kills. There wre not pieces of bodies scattered all over the place, making identification virtually impossible. Pieces of flesh and bone, the rubbish of war, being snatched by dogs who had not been too frightened by the noise of the explosion. Who said there was no such thing as a free lunch? Those opportunist dogs would be all for collateral damage.

Paul felt that his mind was racing ahead again, although he was still writing about the early stages of his life. He wanted to remember it all. This was to be his testament, his confession, his apologia. He intended to send all he wrote by attachment to his own lap-top. From there it would be ready to be sent to newspapers by the press of a button. He would find a way to send it by a mobile phone mail when he got a replacement for the one that had been crushed under the heel of his assailant some days earlier. He would paraphrase Ernie O'Malley's title "On Another Man's Wound" into his own title: "On This Man's Wounds."

Forcing himself to return to childhood memories, Paul could see himself in his mind's eye as a young boy in their local church. His younger brother Morgan was beside him with their mother. His father always stayed outside the chapel door as if he had one foot in and one foot out in so far as religion was concerned. Paul's rosary beads with its white figure of the crucified Christ on a black cross always reminded him of a horse with a white face. He would spend mass-time with the horse galloping across the wooden seat in front of him. He loved the church, even if it was for the wrong reasons. The organ music, the singing, the smell of incense appealed to his various senses. Unlike many who had grown up in his generation he had not found religion to be a weight on his shoulders.

It was to save the world for Christ Paul had gone to Rome with the intention of becoming a priest. It was more likely to save himself from the fires of hell and make sure that he would be on the safe road to heaven. It was a way of staying clean of sin, of avoiding contamination, fornication, adultery or anything else listed in the ten commandments. He wanted to be holy, sinless and pure. In fact he had ended up committing all of the seven deadly sins and a lot more besides. None of that worried him now with the possible exception of the commandment: "Thou shalt not kill."

Paul had grown up at a time in which the Taoiseach or Prime Minister of his country had crossed the floor of the Dáil to vote with the Opposition against the provision of condoms even on prescription. At the same time another part of the country was in turmoil, with bombings and killings the order of the day. There were times when he was in Rome that he would think of getting the next plane home as he heard of prisoners being mistreated, of confessions beaten from prisoners, not to speak of hunger strikes. Many of his colleagues in the Irish College were from the North of Ireland. Talk at mealtimes was seldom about anything other than what was happening there. The fact that they were in a foreign country far from home seemed to magnify every bad news they heard.

Many of those who had studied with Paul were now on the bench of Irish bishops. They seemed to be trusted more than the priests produced by Ireland's largest seminary, Maynooth Safe steady men who had spent time studying in Rome tended to be the bishops of choice as far as the Vatican was concerned. It amused Paul to think that, as he put it in his own mind: "I might now be wearing a red or a purple skirt if I had stuck at it and waited for ordination."

It was during the holidays back home in Ireland that Paul had decided one year not to return to Rome. He was having difficulties with his faith but they did not seem impossible to solve. The attitude of the church to sex, to priestly celibacy and to treating women as second-class citizens annoyed him more, particularly at a time when women seemed closer to emancipation than at any time in the past. He had decided to take a year out, and in fact never really considered returning. There were men dying by the day on hunger strike, and he felt a call stronger than the one to priesthood.

Paul found out before long that he had a particular talent that few others could compete with. He had an extremely accurate shot with a rifle. He had used the shotgun his father had to frighten crows from the corn at home, but had never fired a rifle. One old man had predicted years earlier thet he would be good enough some day for the clay pigeon shooting at the Olympics, but Paul had thought nothing of it. It was not the shooting of clay pigeons that attracted his paramilitary bosses but his possibilities as a sniper. He was brought to South Armagh for a while to learn from the master, but he was not left there for long as his accent would be likely to betray him. Those in charge decided to use him sparingly, but he needed to be completely accurate with his hits. After each operation he was swiftly smuggled across the border.

Paul felt that he had been treated like a little god during his early days in the movement, as his skill became legendary. He had never to drive anywhere. He would be brought to where his target was and back again. He was kept in safe houses. He would be brought somewhere overnight and be back at his office desk in his day-job in the morning. He had to make excuses sometimes, but he let it be known to his fellow employees that he was a bit of a jack-the-lad with a hectic social life. He even boasted one Monday morning that he had made a killing on the previous Saturday, the other workers presuming he had been lucky on the horses.

Paul's skills gradually improved on the word processor, even though he was still typing with one finger. He came to understand that he did not need to put everything in order right away. He could write pieces to use later on and then cut and paste when he was ready. He could change chapters from one place to another if he wanted. This would do away with the little pieces of paper with reminders he had scattered all over the place. It was when looking for something he had written earlier and failing to find it he realised that he was getting tired. It was time to close the lap-top for the night.

He slipped his sore body in beside Adrienne in the bed, wondering would he go straight to sleep or lose himself in her arms. As soon as he felt her warm body beside him, he knew what he wanted. He tried to put his better arm around Adrienne. She turned away from him and told him to: "Fuck off. You choose your writing before me."

xxvi

ADRIENNE WAS UP AND AWAY early the following morning, out of the apartment before Paul awoke. She took her sketchbook with her and took the vaperetto that would be docking closest to Saint Mark's Square. There were few enough tourists there that early in the day, but there was one large Japanese group there before her. The pigeons themselves looked tired and there were not as many of them flying about as when she last visited the place. They probably only came to life really when there were thousands of tourists around throwing them bread and peanuts.

Wondering where the pigeons slept, Adrienne looked around at the roofs os the churches and the galleries and other buildings. For all I know they might just lie down and sleep in the middle of the square, she told herself as she began to sketch some of those which were there, picking at whatever scraps of food they could find on the ground around them. She began to sketch more quickly as other pigeons arrived to join those already there.

Adrienne enjoyed what she was doing, sketching the movements of the pigeons with pencil. She was only half finished each time a pigeon moved away or had a quick contretemps with one of its fellows. Capturing such movements as they happened would help her with later work. She admitted to herself at the same time that she had left her apartment early to teach Paul a lesson. She was going to do as he did, to concentrate on her work more than on their relationship. "Sauce for the goose is sauce for the gander," she told herself.

At the same time she regretted telling him to "fuck off" the previous night. It was crude and unladylike even though it had given her great satisfaction at the time. She knew in her heart of hearts that they should have made love at that moment, or get as near as they could to it, given his injuries. At the same time she felt that he needed to be taught a lesson, that she could not be taken for granted. She was no bimbo that he could have at any time he liked, when he had finished doing something that he considered important. She was a bag of mixed feelings, angry with Paul one minute, pleased that he was writing the next.

When Adrienne got tired sketching the pigeons she headed back towards the landing place from which she could take the vaperetto. There was a great stretch of open sea out in front of her with some islands which seemed to contain churches, or at least buildings with domed roofs. Perhaps they were municipal buildings, she thought. There was a café in front of one of the nearby hotels and she sat on one of the chairs there to have coffee and pizza. She had not eaten breakfast before leaving the apartment as she had not wanted to waken Paul and have to answer his questions. She asked permission of the waiter to sketch what was in front of her. With a dramatic wave of his hand he motioned to her to carry on.

Six or seven gondolas had just arrived with anything from one to four tourists in the beautiful upholstered seats in the centre of each. The gondoliers were competing with each other to get the best places close to the pier, while at the same time appearing to be courteous to each other. Adrienne felt that some of them had great patience in that they did not give rivals a belt of an oar. The gondolas themselves seemed to have the grace of swans as they were manouvered into place by the skill of their handlers. Sketching those movements gave her even more pleasure than drawing the pigeons earlier. The gondolas were slower and more graceful and easier to commit to paper.

Adrienne began to feel awkward because the waiter who had given her permission to sketch was standing behind her, looking over her shoulder. She soon understood why. He offered to buy the sketches from her to put up in the corridors of the building. She replied that they were not finished, and were just preliminary work for future paintings. The man who said he was manager of the café did not have much English, but he managed to communicate his desire to buy the pencil sketches as they were. He would have them framed and 'hanged' as he put it. "How much?"

"A hundred euro each," she answered off the top of her head. She immediately regretted that she had not asked for more money, as he made no attempt to haggle. He just told her he would take eight and wrote her a cheque on the spot. He also said he would like to see the paintings that she based on the sketches. Adrienne explained that they would be abstract, but he said that he would still like to see them when they were finished.

Although she felt somewhat guilty about the way she had treated Paul the night before, Adrienne was not in any hurry home to be with him. He had a lesson to learn. He needed time to work out why she was not there when he awoke that morning. On account of his painkillers he might not even wake up until she returned. What harm? This was her time and she was going to make the best of it. She decided to take a stroll down the back alleys which would surely be safer by day than by night.

Those laneways between high houses or blocks of flats gave her a better idea of how and where the ordinary working people of Venice lived. Many of them seemed to have neither garden or balcony, and there was little growth of any description to be seen except a few flowers in a window-box here and there. These places might be beautiful inside, she thought, but she would certainly hate to live without at least a balcony on which to get some air. Despite her initial enthusiasm she knew now that her stay in Venice was temporary. She had no intention of spending the rest of her life in such confined spaces.

Adrienne came to a large church which no longer functioned as a religious centre, but was now an art and sculpture gallery. There was an exhibition dedicated to model structures based on the drawings of Leonardo Da Vinchi. They were mostly of wood with some metal and canvas, as in his design for what resembled a present day helicopter. Others, based on birdflight were not unlike gliders. What amazed Adrienne most that so many of his designs had to do with the machinery of war, huge catapults for instance that were desined to fire rocks or bombs at or across castle walls. This war-mongery was explained somewhat by a list of names of kings and nobles for whom Leonardo worked.

"I will have to bring Paul to see this," Adrienne said to herself. "He would be interested in Leonardo's cleverness and invention" There were also many line drawings of people's heads, preparatory work for pictures and sculptures. They were as good or better than any such drawing she had studied. The one thing that soured her visit to the exhibition was that the security woman on duty at the door came and told her that she had come in without a ticket. It was a matter of: "Pay up or you will be thrown out." Adrienne felt intimidated as she searched her bag for the ticket while the other woman gesticulated wildly while speaking fast and loudly. Adrienne found her ticket, one that gave entry to most galleries and exhibitions in the city. The security woman grunted ungraciously and franked her ticket with no word of apology or explanation.

xxvii

IT WAS THE RINGING OF the house-phone that awakened Paul that morning. He was surprised that Adrienne was not in the apartment as he staggered from room to kitchen to balcony searching for her. The ringing stopped and he breathed a sigh of relief. It rang again and he allowed it to ring out. He picked it up the third time in case Adrienne might be trying to contact him. The number that showed up on the little screen was a long one, Probably international, he thought, but he answered it anyway.

"Who are you?" he was asked bluntly by a man with an Irish accent.

Paul answered in Italian: "*Non ho capito*," suggesting that he did not understand much English.

"Have you any English at all?" the man at the other end of the phoneline asked. Then he articulated slowly and clearly: "Is Adrienne there? I would like to speak to her."

"Him no here," Paul hoped the man would just hang up. He knew at the same time that Adrienne would be angry if he was rude to one of her friends, or especially to her father.

"Who are you?" the man asked.

"Giorgio. Friend Hadrienne."

"Where is she?"

"You her father?" Paul asked.

"I'm her husband," Patrick answered. "I bet she never told you that she was married."

Paul tried his pidgin English again: "She marry bad man. She divorce."

At this stage Patrick too was resorting to broken English in order to communicate: "No divorce. Separation. Temporary separation. In Ireland five years separation before divorce."

Paul dispensed with the broken English: "Isn't it love that matters in the end and not rules and regulations?"

"Without law we would have anarchy," Patrick answered.

"There is no law or judge or priest able to keep Adrienne and myself apart." Paul was getting satisfaction from having a go at Patricck at this stage.

"We will see about that. Tell her to ring when she gets in."

"I will tell her that her former husband ordered her to ring him back," Paul answered.

"It is not an order," Patrick tried to explain. "This international communication is virtually impossible," he said, as if to himself. "People do not understand what the other peson is saying."

"Don't be fooling yourself about Adrienne," Paul advised him. "She is with me now and she will not be going back to you. You had better get used to that fact."

"We will see," Patrick said smugly. "She might have a different story when she hears what I have to say."

"And what is that?"

"As a matter of courtesy I have to tell Adrienne first," Patrick answered him.

"You've won the lotto?"

"Not that, More important maybe depending on how you look at it."

Paul thought it was time to play dirty: "You've put another young woman up the pole?"

Patrick's anger exploded; "Listen here. What I do or don't do with my life has nothing to do with you. It is between me and Adrienne. You are just a pastime, a gigolo to fill in the time until she is ready to come back to her rightful husband."

"Back to a right bollocks, you mean. A cuckoo that laid an egg in another nest that he was not able to lay in his own."

"You are no Italian," Patrick answeed. "You are as Irish as I am. I will find out all about you. I'll have a private detective on your tail before you know it to find out who and what you really are."

"Do not do that," Paul told him in a menacing voice. "Don't do that, or you will pay very dearly for it."

"Are you threatening me?" Patrick asked. "Are you admitting that you have something to hide?"

"All I am saying is that I would mind my own business if I were you," Paul answered.

"Adrienne is my business, and you have stolen her from me," was Patrick's answer to that.

Paul was tempted to say Patrick had lost his wife as soon as he was unfaithful, but he knew he had gone too far already. Damage limitation was called for. "Look here," he said. "You don't know me and I don't know you. We both love Adrienne in our own way. Why don't we just allow her to decide who she wants to be with?"

Patrick did not seem to take any heed to him: "I will be calling Adrienne later," he said coldly and hung up.

xxviii

Paul did not mention Patrick's phonecall to Adrienne when she returned, as he wanted to find out what kind of humour she was in first. All had been forgiven since the previous night, it seemed, as they ended up in bed together before very long.

They were lying comfortably in each other's arms when Paul casually mentioned: "By the way your ex-husband rang a while ago."

"Patrick?" Adrienne sounded surprised.

"How many ex-husbands have you?" Paul joked.

"I don't have any." Adrienne carressed his chest. "I did have one called Patrick."

"That is the one and he thinks very strongly that he is still your husband."

"Will that man ever learn?"

Paul exaggerated Patrick's attitude as much as he could: "He sounded as if he wanted to have me castrated, hanged, drawn and quartered at the same time. All that stuff about the importance of the marriage vow."

"He was the one to make a mockery of his vows."

"I was tempted to say that," Paul said, "but it was none of my business."

"Adrienne was angry: "He had no right to talk to you like that. Wait until I have a word in his ear."

Paul tried to pour oil on troubled water: "To be fair to him he called looking for you. He was surprised when a man answered. I would not have bothered with answering the phone except that you had disappeared, and I thought that you might have been trying to call me."

"I am too vexed with him to call him back yet. The cheek of him. He was the one who went and screwed that mousy little bitch in the office."

"He said he would call back later," Paul said easily. "I didn't know when you would be back."

"Did he tell you why he was calling?"

"All he said about that was that he wanted to talk to you."

"I hope there is nothing wrong with the baby," Adrienne said.

"I doubt if he would have bothered insulting or threatening me if there was something wrong," was Paul's take on things.

"I'm sorry about that. I'll see to it that it will not happen again."

Patrick sounded as if he did not care about what Patrick had said: "Don't be too hard on him. He has gone through a lot too."

Adrienne gave him a kiss: "You are a right pet. You're heart is in the right place."

Paul went back to work on the lap-top when they had dressed and had a cup of coffee on the balcony. Adrienne had warned him that the second day on such a project was often the hardest.

"A person starts off full of energy and adrenalin, but it is not always easy to maintain."

"It's tiredness more than anything that is affecting me," he said. "My eyes are not used to looking at the screen all day. Not to speak of what happened when you got home."

"That should inspire you?"

"It is not inspiration I need, but for the talk to stop while I am working." Paul explained.

Adrienne gave a little laugh and held her head to one side as if guilty of something. "Ok, I get the message. I will shut up and allow you to get on with your writing."

She took her sketchbook and drawing materials and went out onto the balcony. After flicking through the pigeon sketches she had made that morning she returned and readied a canvas. Paul turned his back so that her movements would not disturb him.

"Would you like an orange juice?" Adrienne asked after a quarter of an hour or so."

"No thanks."

"Would you prefer coffee?"

"I'm pissing coffee."

"What about a glass of wine?"

Paul stood up and still facing away from her, answered: "I don't want orange. I don't want coffee. I don't want wine, and if I do I will go and get it myself so that I will not interfere with your work."

Adrienne saluted mockingly: "Message received loud and clear." She left aside her brush and said: "I am not getting anywhere with this."

Paul stopped writing and asked impatiently: "What is wrong now?"

"I am try to represent gondolas in a symbolic manner and it is just not working for me. I tried the same with pigeons a while ago and I didn't get anywhere with that either."

"Why don't you just ring Patrick and get it over with?" Paul asked.

"What has that to do with anything?"

"You are like a hen on a hot range. There is something annoying you and that is all you can think of."

"I'm not going to call him. I wouldn't give him the satisfaction after the way that he spoke to you."

"Forget about that," Paul answered: "Now if you don't mind would you please let me finish what I have started. We can talk all night after that."

Adrienne raised her hands in apology: "Sorry. Continue. I will not say another word. I promise."

Paul stood up: "I should really do the writing in my own apartment. It would give us both a chance to work without interruption."

"Do whatever you like." Adrienne sounded as he had told her he did not like her company any more."

Just then Patrick rang. Paul went to move the lap-top to the bedroom but Adrienne beckoned him to stay. She covered the receiver with her hand. "I have nothing to say to him that I don't want you to hear."

"Is that fellow still there?" was Patrick's opening remark.

Adrienne decided to make it as difficult as she could for him: "What fellow are you talking about?"

"That ignorant bollocks I was talking to when I rang earlier. I'll bet he didn't even tell you that I rang."

"Do you mean my partner, Paul?" Adrienne asked.

"Georgy is what the liar called himself when I was talking to him. What is his surname?" Paul beckoned to Adrienne not to tell Patrick.

"I don't need a surname for what the two of us get up to," Adrienne answered playfully.

"I didn't like him one bit," Patrick said. He has no manners, no respect."

"We all get jealous from time to time," Adrienne replied.

"This is not jealousy, just contempt. No way is that fellow good enough for you, Adrienne."

Adrienne changed the subject: "How are Sheila and the baby?"

"The baby is good, growing by the day. It was about him that I was trying to ring you this morning."

"What has that to do with me?" Adrienne sensed what was coming.

"His mother says I could see him more often if for instance the two of us were back together again."

Adrienne wanted time to think, to condsider what he was really saying: "By his mother I presume you mean Sheila?" she asked, trying to buy time.

"Isn't that obvious?"

"You mean to tell me that Sheila wants you and me to get back together, after her breaking up our marriage in the first place."

"She is afraid that I mightn't be able to mind the child on my own when I would have him. She wouldn't mind so long as I had a woman with me to mind him."

Adrienne laughed: "What you are really looking for is a skivvy."

"This is not a laughing matter," Patrick said.

"It is the funniest marriage proposal I have ever heard: "Why don't you marry me again so that we can rear my lover's child?"

It's not a marriage proposal because we are married already. We can have the baby from time to time. We wouldn't have to mind him all the time, so you could get on with your painting."

Adrienne did not want to hurt him too much: "You are asking far too much, Patrick," she said.

"I will forgive you everything," Patrick promised.

Adrienne was taken aback: "What would I need forgiveness for?"

"For being with that fellow, Paul or Georgy, or whatever he is called. He sounds like a couple of the Beatles."

"Why don't you go to live in the real world," his former wife told him as she hung up the phone.

Paul did not succeed in writing anything for some time after that, as Adrienne gave out about Patrick and Sheile and everything to do with them. Not only did she not want to go back to him, she said, she did not know why she had ever married him. He was soft, weak and lacked a backbone. She called him one name worse than another, and Sheila worse again. "They would remind you of two constipated skeletons," she said. "They don't have the guts to shite."

Paul laughed: "It will do you good to get that off your chest."

"If he could stiffen his backbone like another part of him, there mght be some rhyme or reason to him."

"You are admitting that he was good at something."

"Good enough to get that one in the family way," Adrienne said, "even though there was not much movement in that department for years before that. The two of us have been together more in the last few days that he was with me for a year. Maybe it was my own fault, that I was not attractive enough for him."

"He must have had a blindfold on if he didn't find you attractive," Paul complimented her.

"Why did he go with that one so?"

"How do I know? Maybe she was easy. Maybe she preferred an older man. She might have some kind of father complex."

Adrienne told him not to go down that road: "It doesn't bear thinking about. I'm sure Freud would have some explanation."

"Poor old Sigmund is blamed for everything," Paul said.

Adrienne was not listening to him: "I wouldn't mind if she was goodlooking, but she is like a little grey mouse. When I say 'grey' I am not talking about the colour of her hair, but of her personality. If that is not to strong a word to associate with her." Adrienne suddenly put her hand to her mouth to stifle a laugh. "God forgve me. Amn't I the right bitch."

"You might have been too strong for him," Paul suggested. "Maybe what he wanted was the kind of mouse you describe."

"The mouse began to roar when she had the baby. The mouse started to lay down the law for Patrick. She doesn't want him now. She just wants his baby, and to rule his life. The little mouse has turned into a rat."

Patrick asked: "have you drawn a picture of that? A mouse metamhorphosing, or whatever you call it, into a rat."

"I didn't but I might yet. It's a great idea. I painted a lot of dark stuff when our marriage was breaking up, but it never occurred to me to paint the one who came between us."

"It could be one way of dealing with your anger."

Adrienne told Paul to get back to his writing, that she would not go on about her marriage any more that day. She would use her paintbrush to deal with it instead.

"Do you know what you should do tomorrow?" she said: "You write in your apartment, and I will paint here. In that way we will not disturb each other. We will be like any two people with separate workplaces.

Paul winked: "And you would never know what might happen when we get home from work."

xxix

PAUL SENT WHAT HE HAD written already by e-mail attachment to his own computer before going to his apartment the following morning. There was a nice clean smell in the place after the work that Adrienne had done with a little help from him earlier in the week. He had a feeling all the same that someone had been in the apartment in the meantime. He could not put a finger on why this was so. It seemed that books on the shelves and other items had been moved slightly. He carefully checked that there was not anybody hiding in the bathroom or in his galley kitchen.

On opening his lap-top Paul wondered was he being paranoid. He had the same feeling as he had about the books and other items. It was as if someone had searched for his passport and failed to find it. It was 'Pól' the Gaelic version of his name, and it would take a lot of guesswork for someone without that language to come up with it. He was pleased to find that the attachment had come through by e-mail and that he was able to open it up and continue his work from where he had left off. He had stopped off in the main shopping street on his way to the apartment and bought a new and expensive phone by which he could send his story to journalists and publicists at the press of a button, if necessary.

Paul's mind was at rest when that much had been done so he began to write. He had decided while on the vaperetto to spend that day writing about his career as a sniper, to tell the whole truth, with names and dates relating to those he had killed. This would help to authenticate his writing, as he had information about some issues that nobody else had. He was not just naming the names of the dead, but of those who had passed on the orders to him. He would love to have known who gave orders from the top but that kind of information never reached him. It didn't matter what was said about some of the leaders, they jusrt denied everything. Others were more honest, they just said sorry and carried on with the pursuit of power.

The question would be asked of course: Why believe an obscure gunman rather than a prominent politician? That was up to the community, to judge one person's explanation against another. Most would know in their hearts who was telling the truth. Killing or violence had not come between many politicians and their voters in a hundred years of Irish politics. Heroes could get away with anything. Paul wrote that he was not in a position to condemn any of them. He had done the same or worse for the same cause.

He took a break from writing after three hours work and walked out slowly and down the stairs one at a time. He had improved a lot as the week went on, but his ribs still hurt him and his legs were stiff and sore. He went to look at his water-taxi, and it seemed to be just as he and Adrienne had left it.

He had an urge to forget about writing and get back to what he did best, bringing tourists around the city. He would need to get back to it soon, he thought, for financial reasons, but the writing was important too. His story needed to be told. The truth might not set him free, but it might help to free others who were in similar situations. He did not know how many of his old comrades had been treated to mock deaths like his. It would be lovely to have a gathering of the living dead sometime, Paul thought, to rake over the ashes of old times

As the day went on Paul had wondered would a knock come to the door signalling the presence of the police investigating the finding of a body at sea. He was used to that kind of feeling. It reminded him of how he used to feel after a hit in his days as a sniper. Despite his care and that of those working with him there was always the danger of being betrayed or spotted or of some basic human error. Police had often the reputation of being slow and ponderous but they were usually thorough, formidible opponents if you got on the wrong side of them.

The Italian Cairbineiri had proven their ability in Southern Italy and Sicily when dealing with the Mafia, despite how practised members of thar group were in keeping silent and not grassing on comrades. He himself had learnt from the masters, those who could sidestep a question with grace and patience and answer another one instead. They were as good at it on radio and television as they were in police stations. While they had considerable political success, Paul felt that it was that slipperiness, that practised evasion that came between them and a political breakthrough in the Irish Republic.

Paul remembered their instructor in those matters, a thin, wiry, nervous looking man with short cropped hair like an American GI in films. He was aware that young idealistic men would have a problem lying, even for the cause. He gave them examples from the Bible, how often Jesus of Naxareth had avoided or dodged questions or just stayed silent during interrogation.

He used answers such as: "Render to Caesar the things that are Caesar's and to God the things that are God's." He would have made a great poitician, the man said. If dodging a question was good enough for Jesus, if it saved him from being crucified sooner than he was, then it was good enough for them as members of the movement. It was good, if cynical psychology, to identify idealistic young men with one of the great idealists of all time.

Paul had his own plan if taken in for questioning. He would be courteous with the first round of questioning and deny everything. If this did not lead to him being freed, he would answer all questions in the Irish language and claim lack of competence in Italian. If an interpreter was brought in he would claim to be a political prisoner, a soldier of the real Irish Republic, that he was protected by the Anglo-Irish Agreement which had been endorsed by the European Community. He would confuse them with constitutional issues and seek help from the Irish diplomatic service. He would do anything and everything except admitting to crime.

Another option was to cut and run, to go back to Ireland using Adrienne as cover, lie low and try to avoid attracting any attention. Right now the safest thing to do was probably to get back to work on the water-taxi and act as normally as possible. The more time that went by without Sandra's body being discovered, the better chance he had.

When he had a lunch of tea and pizza Paul hurried back to his apartment to continue with his writing. Inspired by his thoughts on how to dodge the questions of interrogators, he wrote of the answers of former colleagues in similar situations which had become legendary in the movement. One had claimed that the arms being imported had been delivered by aliens from Mars. Another trained himself to vomit every time he was asked a question. Policemen themselves got physically sick while trying to interview him and eventually ignored him.

As the evening wore on, Paul settled more and more into his writing. There was a big difference between working on his own and trying to write while Adrienne busied herself with her own work. The smallest amount of noise or movement threw him off the track. He was pleased that they had agreed that the best method was for them to work separately and then share the evening together.

Before leaving his apartment Paul arranged a number of items in a way that would tell him if somebody had visited while he was out. He tied threads across the doorway and left his lap-top slightly askew on the desk so that he would recognise if anyone had tried to access what it contained. He sent a copy of what he had written that day to Adrienne's computer, so that he could work on it later if he had time, but more importantly to have a copy available other than in his own word processor.

Paul was not sure if someone had been in the apartment while he was indisposed. If there had been, they had been very careful. He trusted his instincts in matters like that. He had a feeling that he was being watched at a discreet distance, possibly by someone looking for evidence who had not found anything yet. What could he do but watch out for the watchers? As he returned towards Adrienne's apartment on the vaperetto he felt as if he was like many other workers heading home at the end of the day. "If I was in London I would have a bowler hat and an umbrella," he thought, with a shy smile to himself.

XXX

ADRIENNE WAS TIED TO A chair in her apartment. There was a fairly young man with a Northern Irish accent sitting opposite her. She was aware of the handgun in the pocket of his overalls. He asked the same question over and over: "Where is he?"

She gave the same answer again and again: "I don't know."

The young man had been civil so far, and it seemed that he was not really so interested in getting an answer to his question as waiting for Paul to return.

"Are you going to kill him?" Adrienne had asked when he tied her hands behind the back of the chair at first, and assured her that her life was not in danger. She had been on her way from the market with groceries when he walked along beside her and offered to help her with the bags in what seemed like broken Italian. She thought he might be a student trying to earn extra money. She even had a private giggle at the thought this might be one of the gigolos she had been warned about. She would not let him inside the door, but he would be a great help on the stairs.

When they reached the landing she thanked him and reached for her purse to give him a tip. When she looked up he had a gun pointed at her. She offered him her purse, but he said that is not what he wanted but her boyfriend. He directed her to open the apartment door and followed her inside.

"I will wait for him here," he said. "I know he is not here at the moment because I have been trailing him for a few days."

"You should know where he is so," Adrienne replied.

"I have a good idea, but it is safer not to face the lion in his own lair. You will be my cover here."

He did not answer her question about whether he was going to kill Paul, just said that he had nothing against him persnally. He apologised for tying her hands: "I hope I have not hurt you. None of this has anything to do with you. It is quite accidental that you are involved."

"I am involved because I can identify you," Adrienne said.

"I would have worn a balaclava," he joked, "but that might have attracted attention on the street."

Adrienne was afraid, but she felt the best chance to escape was to warn Paul by speaking loudly and having him realise there was someone with her in the apartment. The trouble was that she did not know at what time he waould return. The best thing to do was to keep talking: "You have to kill me. I am a witness."

"Shut up," he said bluntly. "Nobody said anything about killing anyone."

Adrienne spoke in an even louder and frightened voice: "I know you are going to kill us, but you don't have to. I have money. I own a house. I will buy off the contract. I'll sign over a house in Wicklow to you."

"If I was interested in money or houses do you think I would be here?" he asked. "I'm here for the cause, the cause of Ireland, like your boyfriend was once." He tried to reassure her: It doesn't matter that you have seen me, because you will never see me again. I'll see to that."

"By killing me?" Adrienne asked.

"By making sure that our paths never cross."

"What has Paul done to deserve this?"

"Nothing. He is surplus to requirements. He is a source of embarrassment to the movement."

"Are you not afraid that you will be discarded in the same way in a few years time?" Adrienne asked.

"The war is over," was the man's answer. "There are a few loose ends to be tied up."

So Paul is just a loose end?"

The man shrugged.

"What about the information he has stashed away? What about the documents that are to be opened after his death?"

The man frowned as if this was an unexpected fly that had landed in his ointment: "Where are those?"

Adrienne shook her head: "In a Bank as far as I know, or with a solicitor. But don't worry about that. All you have to do is to kill him, or kill both of us. Let someone else deal with the shit when it hits the fan."

The man took a mobile phone from his pocket, and said with heavy irony to Adrienne: "Stay there. Don't go anywhere." He went over near the balcony and spoke to someone on the phone in a low tone in Gaelic. Adrienne could only make out some of what he was saying, but she knew that she had put a cat among the pigeons by mentioning the information Paul had stashed away. It was then that she heard Paul's key in the lock and she shouted: "No."

The phone was dropped as the man opened the door. Adrienne could hear Paul trying to shuffle down the stairs. Then there were shots.

xxxi

ADRIENNE WAS DESPERATELY TRYING TO free her hands when Paul staggered through the door. A red bloodstain was spreading on his shirt close to his left shoulder. He stood with his back to the door in a way that reminded her of the statue of the dying Cuchulainn in Dublin's GPO.

"I got him," he said, before collapsing on the floor. The mobile phone in his pocket started to ring. Almost immediately people started to come through the doorway of the apartment, police, medics, people from other parts of the building. Someone freed her hands but they were numb. People were speaking to Adrienne in Italian and English, but she found it difficult to decipher what they were saying. All of her focus was on Paul. Was he going to live or to die? A kind policewoman went on her knees beside her, reassured her Paul was still alive, that she had felt his pulse.

"Is he your husband?" the policewoman asked.

"He is," answered Adrienne, in case she would not be allowed in the ambulance with him.

"Why was he carrying a gun?" the policewoman asked when they were in the ambulance.

"A long story."

"Drugs?"

"Politics," Adrienne answered.

"Al Quaeda?"

"IRA. The full story is on his lap-top," Adrienne said. "I can't deal with that now that he is between life and death."

The Policewoman touched her hand. "I understand. There will be plenty of time to talk about that."

Adrienne's heart soared when Paul opened his eyes as he was carried from the sea-ambulance. He half-raised himself on one elbow, looked at her and smled. She knew when he fell back that he had breathed his last.